‖‖‖ W9-APH-959

"NOW WHAT ARE YOU DOING?"

Katherine all but gasped as he removed his cravat and opened the top button of his shirt. She stared at him, obviously fascinated. He flexed his muscles as if in a stretch and her eyes widened. Hiding a grin, he bent to heft the timber onto his shoulder.

"Lead on," he told her.

She skittered out of the carriage house as if the building were on fire. He followed her into the house and up the stairs to the sitting room, where he set the plank down. There were no musicians in sight. Instead, conspicuous under the windows was a neat platform draped in white.

"Fancy that," he said. "You didn't need this after all. Maybe you'd like me to carry it back down for you."

"Yes, perhaps that would be best," she agreed, swallowing.

He bent to pick up the beam and paused, then rose, staring at his shoulder. "Now look there. I've gone and dirtied my shirt. Perhaps I should remove that as well, before I get more dust on it."

She swallowed again. "Yes, perhaps you should."

The minx. She was still enjoying herself. He rolled his shoulders and watched her catch her lower lip with her teeth. And such a nice lower lip it was—rounded, rosy, tender. Before he knew it, he closed the distance between them and pulled her into his arms. . . .

Other Works by Regina Scott

The Unflappable Miss Fairchild

The Twelve Days of Christmas

"Sweeter Than Candy" in
A Match for Mother

The Bluestocking on His Knee

"A Place by the Fire" in
Mistletoe Kittens

Catch of the Season

A Dangerous Dalliance

The Marquis' Kiss

"The June Bride Conspiracy" in
His Blushing Bride

The Incomparable Miss Compton

The Irredeemable Miss Renfield

Utterly Devoted
(coming in August 2002)

LORD BORIN'S SECRET LOVE

Regina Scott

ZEBRA BOOKS
Kensington Publishing Corp.
http://www.kensingtonbooks.com

ZEBRA BOOKS are published by

Kensington Publishing Corp.
850 Third Avenue
New York, NY 10022

Copyright © 2002 by Regina Lundgren

All rights reserved. No part of this book may be reproduced in any form or by any means without the prior written consent of the Publisher, excepting brief quotes used in reviews.

If you purchased this book without a cover you should be aware that this book is stolen property. It was reported as "unsold and destroyed" to the Publisher and neither the Author nor the Publisher has received any payment for this "stripped book."

All Kensington titles, imprints, and distributed lines are available at special quantity discounts for bulk purchases for sales promotions, premiums, fund-raising, educational or institutional use.

Special book excerpts or customized printings can also be created to fit specific needs. For details, write or phone the office of the Kensington Special Sales Manager: Kensington Publishing Corp., 850 Third Avenue, New York, NY 10022. Attn. Special Sales Department. Phone: 1-800-221-2647.

Zebra and the Z logo Reg. U.S. Pat. & TM Off.

First Printing: May 2002
10 9 8 7 6 5 4 3 2 1

Printed in the United States of America

To managing females everywhere,
especially Gariann Gelston and Christa Knudson

One

Alexander Wescott, Viscount Borin, leaned back in the leather armchair of the Marquis of Hastings's private office in Whitehall. He pulled out the pocket watch from his tastefully embroidered celestial blue waistcoat and flipped open the gold filigree case. But he did not consult the time. His gaze never left the man behind the desk.

Lord Hastings gave no clue as to his thoughts. The marquis's deep brown eyes remained on the papers on the claw-foot walnut desk before him, one hand stroking his walrus mustache. Alex felt the seconds ticking off. He heard young Captain Randolph, who stood guard behind the marquis, shift impatiently in his Oxford blue regimentals.

"An interesting account, Borin," Lord Hastings said at last. "I imagine it was rather entertaining to discover you were being followed."

The tone was characteristically chipper, but Alex wasn't fooled. Under the well-cut navy coat and dapper demeanor beat the heart of England's spy master, a heart after his own, he hoped. He snapped shut his watch and replaced it without rumpling his dove gray morning coat. "I rather hoped you would find it interesting," he told Hastings, "given the rumors circulating about the *ton*."

Hastings raised a brow as iron gray as his short-cropped hair. "That nonsense about a French spy infiltrating society?"

"Is it nonsense?" Alex pressed, planting his boots firmly in the thick blue carpet. "It seems to me I have seen your men more in London than ever in the past. Rumor has it that you suspect one of the beau monde of sharing secrets."

The captain's dark eyes lighted, but Hastings leaned back with a small smile on his lips. "What I suspect and what is real may be two different things, my boy. It is no secret I recruit my agents from among the aristocracy. It is also no secret that none of them would be easily induced to part with information. If there is a spy circulating at the London balls this Season, he is no doubt merely looking for a wealthy heiress to subsidize his activities."

Alex tried not to look disappointed. "But surely you need additional men to chase down these cursed rumors. I offered to join you last March. I repeat my request to be of service. The fact that I am being followed should be proof to you that someone suspects I already belong to your staff."

Hastings met his gaze at last, and Alex nearly flinched at the sympathy in the man's eyes. "I said it was interesting that you are being followed, my boy. However, I would suspect it has more to do with your gambling or flirting than your attraction to espionage."

Blood roared in his ears. Alex surged to his feet. "Do you impugn my honor, sir? Give me the names of your seconds."

Randolph squared powerful shoulders and stepped forward menacingly even as Hastings sighed. "Oh, do sit down, Borin. It is entirely this sort of thing that makes you unsuited to the Service."

As quickly as the temper had come, it left him. Alex sank back upon the chair. "I beg your pardon, sir," he replied with a formal nod. "But if you knew what this appointment means to me . . ."

Hastings sighed again. "I understand. You are thoroughly bored with the entertainments of London and you were never the type to rusticate in the country. But it does not follow that espionage will be your salvation."

Alex leaned forward, eager to make his case. "But I know I would be good at it. I am an excellent swordsman and a bruising fighter—ask Gentleman Jackson. No horse has been born that I cannot ride, no vehicle built I cannot drive. I speak, read, and write French, Italian, and Spanish. And I am a dab hand at acting."

The spy master smiled. "Yes, I had heard you hung about Drury Lane rather frequently, but I thought it had more to do with a certain beautiful opera dancer than improving your military skills."

Alex willed himself not to react, but the captain's grin was catching. He gave it up and grinned back.

"Very well," he allowed, "I admit it. But my dedication to my previous pursuits should prove to you my determination. Whatever I have set my hand to flourishes. Yet I am stagnating. I need a new challenge. Will you not accept my services?"

That irritating sympathy never left the older man's eyes. He pushed the papers away from him, and Alex's heart sank. "Forgive me, but I must decline. I have known you since you were in leading strings. You have a heart for adventure, Alex, but no stomach for hard work. Things have been too easy for you to have developed the trait of persistence, I suspect. Find a nice girl, settle down, and manage your estates."

Alex rose and offered him a bow. "Your servant, sir. I must, of course, respect your decision. However, you are wrong about me, and I hope to someday prove it to you."

He refused to meet Captain Randolph's gaze as he walked stiffly from the office.

Once outside the building, he faltered. What was he to do now? The future yawned bleak before him. Was he such a care-for-nothing that no one could believe he was useful?

He straightened his sagging shoulders and forced himself to stroll up the street with his usual ennui. He would let no one see how much the blow hurt. Refused by the War Office, not once, but twice! And this while England begged for soldiers to fight Napoleon. He passed around Whitehall for Pall Mall and could not suppress a shudder at the sight of a captain leading in a group of raggedy men for recruits. There was always room in the infantry, if he could stomach the work. Surely there were better ways to entertain himself.

But what if not the Service? His personal affairs needed no attention. His estate in Hampshire was run by an experienced, honest, capable steward. He had no interest in assisting. The few times Alex had sat in with him, the discussions of enclosures, rents, and pasturage had gone in one ear and out the other.

His town house was run by an equally capable butler, his stables by a consummate master of horse. He did, of course, pick his own mounts at Tattersall's, but he left the care, feeding, and training thereof to more experienced hands. As long as the horse was fast and did not clash with his riding jacket, he did not question his horse master's decisions.

No more did he need to dabble in the Exchange. His considerable fortune was managed by an astute financier. He was vaguely aware that he was invested in a number of activities, such as rubies in India and sailing ships in the Caribbean. It seemed he might even own an estate in Canada of all places. As long as he had funds when he needed them, he saw no reason to meddle.

He also didn't feel particularly useful in political circles. He had tried to do his duty in Parliament, but the endless speeches dulled his mind and most of the measures seemed petty or of little use to anyone. The intrigue of trying to convince various members to vote for a particular measure was mildly interesting, but who could stand to compete with a high stickler like Castlereagh or the mindless chatter of Sally Jersey?

At one time he had even tried to do something to improve the country. After hearing of several worthwhile charities, he'd gone to a meeting of the Society for the Prevention of Cruelty to Climbing Boys. Unfortunately, while he had endowed their cause with a sizable donation, he could not find it in himself to sit week after week and discuss the burning and maiming of children.

No more could he stand to simply return to his previous pursuits. One could only win so many carriage races. Chas Prestwick currently held the record in that arena anyway, and he had no reason to challenge his friend. Gambling was of no interest when one could be virtually assured of winning. And while he could not deny a certain attraction to the ladies, even the attentions of the delightful Miss Lydia Montgomery, his current mistress, had begun to cloy.

Perhaps Hastings was right—life was too easy for him. He had excelled in school, on the practice fields, and in the ballrooms. Too many other pursuits were simply boring. He felt as if there were a vacuous hole in his life, sucking him down. All the more reason to take on a new challenge.

And what better challenge than to embrace the duties of an agent for the king? He could easily imagine dodging behind enemy lines, seducing duchesses for vital information, and daringly eluding capture to return the information to England. There were those who would consider such exploits as beneath a gentleman, but he could see how vital the role was to defeating the Corsican monster. Wellington's war on the Peninsula could only accomplish so much if military information was already in the hands of the enemy. The French were notorious for their use of secret agents to ferret out England's most closely held information.

He shook his head as he turned down Pall Mall. He would not be the one to stop them. Hastings had been clear in his refusal. He thought Alex a wastrel. What a conundrum! His wastrel life was entirely what he hoped to change! He had thought surely the fact that he was being followed would be sufficient for the old boy to reconsider his case.

The problem had started several weeks ago, shortly after the opening of this 1813 Season. For the last year he had taken to walking from diversion to diversion. His coachman complained of boredom and his valet lamented the wear on his boots, but what could one do? A man could not count on a vehicle or animal for transportation behind enemy lines. He needed to be fit to join the Service. He already boxed twice a week and fenced three times. Walking provided additional exercise and kept him limber. Occasionally a friend would raise a brow at his habit—none of them were willing to soil their slippers; however, most people paid him no attention. Perhaps that was why he had noticed when he developed an extra shadow.

Sometimes it was a shabbily dressed man, hat pulled down to shade his face. Other times it was an urchin boy with a gamin grin. Whichever, they clung to his heels like bottom mud from a country stream. Twice he had attempted to give chase, and both times they had eluded him. He would have thought them no more than footpads except his staff had reported them hanging about the mews as well. He was being watched.

But to what purpose? He could not deny that he had hoped it had something to do with his earlier offer to support the War Office. Perhaps the enemies of the Crown did not know he had been refused. He had been rather pleased they thought him intriguing enough to follow. It was nothing but annoying to think it had something to do with his current life instead.

Yet he could not see how. For all his exploits, he was a gentleman. He paid his debts promptly and never dallied with married ladies or unwilling lasses. He never cheated or lied or stole. And he liked to think his physique was muscular enough to deter common thieves. In short, he could think of no reason why anyone would wish to spy on him.

He was halfway down St. James when he saw his shadow again. It was the boy this time. Glancing back, Alex saw him dart behind a lorry as if to avoid detection. So, they were still after him. He should alert Bow Street. If the War Office couldn't be bothered, at least the magistrates might look into the matter. Yet after his refusal by Hastings, Alex was in no mood to ask anyone's assistance. He started back to try to catch the boy once again himself, then hesitated.

He had threatened to prove to Lord Hastings that he was wrong. Alex was capable of working hard, however distasteful he found the prospect. What if, instead of merely catching the lad, he managed to follow the boy to his master? What if he uncovered whatever nefarious scheme they hoped to enact? If it had anything to do with the spy in society, so much the better.

Wouldn't that prove to Hastings that he was worthy to join the Service?

He tipped his hat to a passing lady as if that had been his intent in turning all along. She regarded him with an interested smile, but he turned before she could question him. Then he sauntered up the street and around the corner. With a quick glance back, he saw the boy follow.

He led the lad a merry chase, turning first one direction, then another. Finally, he spotted a shop with a large front window. He ducked inside and stood back from the light, watching. His pursuer stood just outside, glancing in all directions. Up close, the boy looked to be about eight, with a none-too-clean round face and eyes that were narrowed in concentration. A dusty cap hid all but the fringes of his hair, which looked to be a deep auburn. Alex held his breath as the boy's shoulders sagged in obvious defeat. The lad turned to go.

"Might I assist you, sir?" a young female shop worker asked politely. Glancing quickly back at her, he took note of his surroundings. Lacy corsets and dainty chemises decorated the walls and sewing forms. Every person, from the patrons to the shopkeeper, was female, and all of them were staring at him with various degrees of amusement, shock, or disapproval. He tipped his hat to them and hurried after the boy.

He did his best to be inconspicuous. It wasn't difficult in the shopping district. He had never realized just how many tall, blond gentlemen strolled about in dove gray morning coats and black trousers. He'd have to speak to his tailor about something more original. For now, he was thankful to blend in so well. The boy scurried along as if he had no idea he was being followed. He even had the temerity to skip when the cobblestones became more even. The few times he glanced back, Alex was careful to duck out of sight.

He fully expected the lad to detour toward a seedier part of town, and was surprised when he at last made his way down the alley behind a set of modest town houses at the edge of Mayfair. With bold-faced impudence, he jumped a short kitchen gate and scurried up the walk to enter one of the houses. Had the rascal been hired by someone of the *ton,* then? Alex waited for a moment, but the boy did not return. Surely this was the boy's home. He had located the lair of his nemesis. Anticipation curled in his stomach. Oh, he was definitely made for this. All he had to do was catch the culprits and Lord Hastings would have to admit as much.

Yet he couldn't simply stride up to the back door and demand the boy. He could scarcely expect the kitchen staff to give him up so easily. He rather thought criminals protected their own, if only to prevent them from telling tales to the magistrates. He'd have to try something else.

He counted the number of houses from the corner, then hurried back around the terrace. He had to learn who owned the house and whether they knew their pot boy or stable boy had been spying. It was possible someone else had hired the boy, or that he held more than one job. The only way to learn more was to meet the owners of the house. He could decide from there how much information to provide them, and how much he could weasel out of them. He had to restrain himself from rubbing his hands together with glee.

From the front, the house looked no different from others along the street—three floors of windows and a door to the left. It did not look like a den of iniquity. The steps were clean swept, the trim in good repair. Perhaps he had been misled after all.

He nearly turned back, but decided to knock just in case. As he approached the entry, however, he could not help but hear a commotion inside. His hand raised to knock, he paused. Doors slammed, voices shouted.

What on earth had he gotten himself into?

Excitement surged through him, and he rapped sharply at the door.

Two

A few moments earlier, Katherine Collins had heard the sound she had been waiting for all afternoon.

"I shall kill him!" her uncle thundered.

Katherine exchanged glances with her stepsister Constance Templeman, who rose from the leather-bound chair in the library in a flurry of pink-sprigged muslin. Katherine gathered up her own navy skirts and hurried after her for the corridor. Already their man, Bixby, and their cook and housekeeper, Emma, were hustling from below stairs.

"Places," Katherine ordered from long experience.

Heavy-set Emma grabbed Constance's hand, and they scurried for the kitchen stair. Bixby took his place by the front door as Katherine started up the main stairs.

Above them, the door to her uncle's study slammed. "I tell you, I shall kill him this time," Sir Richard Collins swore, storming onto the landing. His handsome face was florid, his cravat loose over his dark coat, as if he had yanked the linen free in his frustration. "Bixby, fetch my sword cane!"

He started down the polished stairs, his limp barely evident. Katherine put herself squarely in his path.

"Whatever is the matter, Uncle?" she asked, making

her eyes as wide as possible. A shame that her gray eyes were not nearly as vapid and innocent as Constance's or her heavy auburn tresses as light and curly as her stepsister's blond mane. But her dainty stepsister would be far more convincing in the role Katherine had given her to play. Constance could never confront anyone, even to save the family from social ruin. In the Collins house, Katherine was the managing female.

"Stand aside, Katherine," her uncle blustered, though she was thankful that he was not so far gone as to touch her on the stair, lest she fall. "That editor of *The Morning Chronicle* has gone too far this time. How dare he malign Wellington's strategies?"

Katherine refused to give way. "I am certain Mr. Perry means no disrespect for the valiant general, Uncle. Perhaps if you read the piece on the Peninsular War again . . ."

"Again!" Her uncle's brown eyes, almond shaped like her own, glared down at her. "I couldn't stand to finish it once, let alone twice. Now move out of my way or I'll have Bixby confine you to your room for a week."

She was fairly sure Bix would never follow through on such an order. He knew which way the wind blew in their house. Besides, he was more grandfather than butler, and just as likely to spoil her. Unfortunately, she was even more sure her uncle would not be swayed by logic. Sighing dramatically, she moved out of his way and watched as Bixby flawlessly executed the second phase of their plan.

"Will you be wanting a carriage, then, Sir Richard?" the elderly retainer asked as he handed her uncle his top hat. He was so diffident that Katherine wondered whether Sir Richard would notice. Bixby and her uncle had been campaigners together. There were times when neither remembered who was master and who servant.

She shook her head sharply behind her uncle's back to warn Bix not to play it too brown, but Sir Richard was already blustering ahead.

"Of course I want a carriage," he snapped as she came down the stairs to help. "Do you expect me to walk? I took a ball for Britain, blast you. Must I do everything else as well?"

Bixby's blue gaze met hers, and she was pleased that he did not deign to answer the question. He'd been there when her uncle had been wounded. Sir Richard would never have gotten home without him. Most days, Sir Richard remembered that and was thankful.

Bixby straightened his thin shoulders and looked down his long nose. "If you'll be so good as to wait in the library, then, sir," he said in his best imitation of a stiff-rumped butler, "I shall fetch you a hack."

"Wait?" Sir Richard glared at him, and Katherine thought Bix had given away the game. But her uncle merely snatched the ebony cane from Bixby's long-fingered grip. "Oh, very well. But be quick about it. And this isn't my sword cane."

"No, sir," Bixby replied, carefully snagging the offending implement as Sir Richard waved it angrily about. "I shall do my best to locate it."

"I believe I saw it upstairs in my brother's room, Bixby," Katherine offered. "Eric is rather fond of playing adventurer."

The butler nodded and started for the stairs. Sir Richard ripped the cane from his hands as he passed.

"Never mind! I'll use this one. Mad as I am, I can likely kill him with my bare hands. And you can forget about that carriage. My indignation will carry me."

Bixby and Katherine exchanged glances. So much for phase two. Her butler pulled down the front of his brown wool coat in resignation and raised his voice to start the third phase.

"Will that be all, then, sir?"

Before Sir Richard could answer, there came a crash from the stair to the kitchen and a blood-curdling scream. Emma burst out the door, large hands wringing before her frilly white apron, white-streaked blond hair flying. Her jowls quivered on either side of her rosebud mouth.

"Oh, mercy on us! Miss Constance be fallen! Help her, Sir Richard, do!"

Her uncle blanched. Leaning heavily on his cane, he hurried down the short corridor for the servants' stair. Katherine and Bixby fell into step behind him. Emma held open the door and Katherine peered down around her uncle.

As usual, Constance was the weak link in their plan. She either balked at playing a role, or played it far beyond the limits of normality. Today, she lay on the landing below them, skirts tastefully draped about her sprawled limbs, golden curls fanning out behind her head. Unfortunately, her head was cocked at such a convincingly horrid angle that she wrung a gasp from her uncle. Her creamy complexion was so pale that if it hadn't been for the rise and fall of her well-molded bosom, Katherine also might have thought her gravely injured. The fact that Eric had returned from his task for the day and stood below her staring wide-eyed only completed the ghastly picture.

"Dear God," Sir Richard breathed out, scrambling down the stairs. "What happened?"

"I didn't do it," Eric declared, sidling around his uncle, who knelt to touch the girl's cheek.

Constance's blue eyes fluttered open, and Katherine mouthed a warning behind her uncle's back for her stepsister to behave. Before she could see the effect of her caution, her brother flew up the steps and she caught him to her.

"Of course you didn't do anything to harm Constance, Eric," she said, giving him a look of warning as well. "You only just returned from the errands I commissioned. Good thing you are home early. We can send you for the carriage so Uncle can visit the office of *The Chronicle*."

Emma put a plump hand on Katherine's shoulder as if in agreement. The boy's mouth widened in an O and she knew he understood them. He should have been as relieved as her uncle to hear Constance moan theatrically. Instead, he paled and tugged on her hand to lead her away from Emma and out of the stairwell. She didn't like missing the next act of their little play, but she did want to hear what he had to say. She could only hope her stepsister wouldn't overplay her hand while Katherine was gone.

"I didn't know Uncle would be up so soon," her brother said when they were out of earshot of the drama in the stair. "I thought he'd sleep to all hours after drinking so much last night."

Katherine shook her head. "Even with the drink his wound troubles him too much to lay abed for long, I fear. He threatened to kill Mr. Perry again. But our latest plan seems to be working. Constance will get him safely upstairs and keep him at her bedside until we are assured the offices are closed for the day."

Eric pulled off the cap and ran a hand back through hair as thick and auburn as her own. "Are you sure this will work?"

She smiled down at him, watching his button nose wrinkle his freckles into a solid mass of cinnamon. "It will work. Do my plans ever fail?"

A sharp rap at the door belied her confidence.

Eric grabbed her hand. "It's him! I knew I could get him to follow me home."

"Him?" Katherine knew she had blanched. "Oh, Eric, no! Is that Lord Borin?"

Her brother nodded, tugging her toward the door. "Yes, it must be. You said it was time for him to meet Constance again. I got him here for you."

Katherine resisted him even as the rap sounded again. "I said we were *nearly* ready. There is still much we do not know about him. And this is the worst possible time. I jolly well can't have him meet Constance when she's supposed to be gravely injured!"

Eric paused. "Oh, yes, there is that. Well, maybe if we ignore him, he'll go away."

The third rap was far too determined to indicate that their visitor would go away anytime soon. Katherine frowned. They had worked too hard to identify and attract Viscount Borin to simply let him slip through their fingers now. He might not be able to meet Constance, but she couldn't let him leave without furthering her cause. She grabbed Eric and pushed him toward the servants' stair. "Keep them busy until I send him away. Then tell Bix what's happened."

With a nod, Eric scampered off.

Katherine hurried to the front door and snatched it open. The gentleman standing there was obviously expecting trouble. His eyes were narrowed and his lean shoulders were so tense that she wondered he didn't rip free from the close-fitting gray coat. She had to admit, however, that his air of expectancy in no way detracted from his charm. His hair was nearly as golden as her stepsister's, though not as wavy, being modestly cut around his oval face. He had high cheekbones and a determined chin. It was a manly face, a face a sculptor would love, with well-shaped angles and planes. But by far his best feature was his deep-set vivid blue eyes ringed by golden lashes. No woman could resist him, she was certain. What an excellent choice she'd made for Constance.

She nearly sighed aloud with pleasure, but realizing that would ruin all, she merely hid her delight beneath a deep curtsy. "Good afternoon, sir. Our servants are busy at the moment. I am the lady of the house. How might I assist you?"

She rose to watch him, and marveled at how easily she read his emotions from his face. The quirk of his firm lips told her he knew he was at a disadvantage. A puff of a sigh informed her he wasn't sure what to do about it. She could understand his dilemma. The rules of polite society dictated that a gentleman could not simply introduce himself to a lady. She decided to make it easy for him and achieve her own purposes in the process.

"Most likely you are here to see my stepsister, Constance Templeman. Any number of gentlemen visit for that reason. When one is the belle of the Season, one must expect adulation, I suppose."

His brow cleared. "Yes, that is exactly why I am here. Miss Templeman. Might I have a moment of her time?" He smiled.

My, what a charming smile, Katherine thought. The light shone from eyes bluer than a late-afternoon sky, and the ends of his mouth curled up in the most beguiling manner. She fancied she even saw the beginnings of a dimple near one corner of his lips. Surely this was one suitor Constance wouldn't refuse. Perhaps they might yet keep her stepsister's fortune in hand. There were six weeks left until her twentieth birthday, after all.

But the stunning gentleman on her front step must never know that he had been chosen for the role of husband to the fair Constance. He needed to think courting Constance was all his idea. Katherine had found that gentlemen preferred it that way. Indeed, they tended to become quite irrational if they thought they were being manipulated. Unfortunately, they weren't tremendously rational even when they were in charge. Look at her uncle. Look at her father. Look at the toad who had inherited from her stepfather. Their sheer incapability to care for their families was one of the reasons she so often had to arrange matters herself.

Like now.

She gave him back what she hoped was a charming smile. It would never match his for beauty. She was not her stepsister, after all. He'd have to make do with her plainer features, darker hair, and thinner body. But it did her heart good to see that he didn't seem to mind. His smile deepened along with hers.

"I fear my stepsister is indisposed just now," she replied. "If you would leave your card, I am certain she would be delighted to make your acquaintance another time."

The thumps behind her told her Constance would shortly be making a rather unflattering appearance, if she was capable of doing anything in an unflattering manner. Still, Katherine could not take chances. One of the things they had learned about Lord Borin was that he didn't seem to like things too difficult. Constance must be a challenge, but never a trial. Katherine held out her hand expectantly.

"Perhaps I might speak with Lord Templeman," her paragon said with remarkable stubbornness. She'd have to add that to the wall. None of the data they'd gathered so far had indicated he was stubborn. Quite the contrary. Eric and Bix had been following him for several weeks and had made any number of inquiries. They had talked with his friends, his relations, even his old nurse. Katherine had carefully arranged all the data on the wall of a little-used room in the attic. According to that information, everyone thought him even tempered and complacent, quite the polished London gentleman. That was one of the reasons she had chosen him over the other fellows they had considered. That and the fact that he was one of the few men for whom Constance had actually shown a fancy.

And he was so terribly adorable.

There was another thump and a squeal that sounded suspiciously like Eric. Her Adonis attempted to peer around her, and she stood on tiptoe to block his view, afraid that he still could look over her head. She knew her smile was strained.

"Lord Templeman does not live here," she explained. "My stepfather, the former Lord Templeman, died several years ago. My uncle, Sir Richard Collins, is our guardian."

"Sir Richard, then," he said agreeably, but she heard the determination in his voice. She also heard the stair door bump open and the murmur of sympathetic voices.

"Indisposed," she snapped. "Your card, sir?"

He also stood on tiptoe, leaning to the left. "Will he be available tomorrow?"

She pulled the door farther closed against her to prevent him from seeing more than the top of the stair. Behind her, she heard Bixby call caution and her uncle's voice answer sharply.

"Yes, fine," she barked out. "Three o'clock. Good day, Lord Borin."

And she snapped shut the door before he could argue.

Three

Alex blinked as the door snapped shut. Singular woman. He found himself intrigued, and he didn't even know her name.

But she evidently knew his. Of course, he was a common fixture in social circles, so it wasn't entirely surprising she would recognize him. What was more surprising was that he didn't recognize her. He thought he knew every pretty girl who'd been out the last few Seasons, if only so he could avoid their matchmaking mamas.

Of course, she wasn't in the common way, he reflected as he descended the stair. Her thick coil of auburn hair nearly dwarfed her elfin face. The dress she wore had been severe enough for a governess, but the clean lines somehow drew his attention to her slender curves. She was also petite, coming only to his collarbone if one counted the knot of hair on top of her head. She looked as insubstantial as eiderdown and far too young to be the lady of the house for her stepsister Miss Templeman. She did look old enough, however, to be ready for marriage. Yet there had been no wedding band on that slender finger.

Unfortunately, for all she intrigued him, she hadn't been very helpful. He knew little more about the household than when he had followed his shadow here. But he had twenty-four hours. What could an enterprising gentleman learn in that time? Setting his top hat at a jaunty angle, he set forth to find out.

It was evening before Katherine had a moment to consider her next steps in her plan for her stepsister. First she made sure Sir Richard was kept busy with Constance as she rested from her "accident."

"Why do I feel you had a hand in this, Colonel?" he asked Katherine when she slipped into the bedroom she shared with her stepsister to check on them.

She smiled at his pet name for her. "Do you think I would trip my dearest stepsister down the stairs, Uncle? Besides, I was with you at the time, if you recall."

"I recall. I also recall my intentions at the time. A simple word of warning would have been sufficient, girl. You need not cozen me into doing the right thing."

She did not point out that she had tried to stop him with words. He had not been in a mood to recognize subtlety. Besides, she knew her attempts to manage things annoyed him. But if he wouldn't take responsibility for the family, what else was she to do?

Now was no exception. She had thought Constance might keep him safely by her side. All too soon, however, he complained of the pain in his leg and hobbled off to his study. Certain of what her uncle intended, Katherine intercepted Bixby on his way up with a tray. She raised a brow at the crystal decanter.

"Watered down two to one, just like you ordered," her man promised with a nod of his balding head. "And Emma has Yorkshire pudding in the oven, Sir Richard's favorite."

Katherine returned the nod. "Good. Perhaps if we

can fill his stomach with food, he will have no room for the liquor."

"Worth a try," Bixby replied. "Don't you give up on him now, Miss Katherine. He's just fallen into a funk. Pride of the regiment, your uncle was once. Wasn't a man in the unit who wouldn't have traded places with him."

"I know," Katherine murmured. "Perhaps once we've gotten Constance safely wed we can turn our attentions to finding him something more worthwhile to pursue than the fastest way to empty a whiskey bottle. In the meantime, when you're done with Sir Richard, and Emma is free, join me in our bedchamber, will you? We shall need several new plans if Mr. Perry continues his attacks on Wellington."

"I wish Sir Richard would just read another paper," her man muttered, but he hurried off to complete his duties.

Katherine could not argue with him. Unfortunately, she'd already tried that tack. Her uncle insisted on *The Chronicle*. The few occasions when it had failed to appear on their doorstep he had stomped out to find a copy. They had to try something else to keep him from maiming the good editor.

But when they all gathered in the bedchamber, Katherine discovered that no one had any other ideas.

"Mayhap we should let him go to *The Chronicle*," Emma suggested, absently twining a piece of her coarse braided hair around one plump finger as she sat on the bed Katherine shared with her stepsister. "Seems like if that editor be so foolish as to bad-mouth General Wellington, he ought to be expecting a poke in the nose for his trouble."

"Uncle doesn't intend to punch him," Eric told her from where he was curled up at the foot of the bed. "He wants to run him through."

"Surely he wouldn't murder Mr. Perry," Constance protested from the head of the bed, one hand clutching the gold cross she wore about her neck. " 'Let not the sun go down on your wrath,' Ephesians four: twenty-six."

Bixby shook his head, leaning back against the wood-wrapped fireplace. "Sir Richard's not a vengeful man, but he isn't himself when he's been drinking. Still, he is full grown. Perhaps Emma has the right of it—we should stop interfering."

Constance and Emma nodded sagely. Eric looked thoughtful. Perched beside him, Katherine stared at them.

"Have you all considered what would happen if he disgraces himself outside this house?" she scolded. "He would be mortified when he came to his senses. He might even go deeper into this decline. Not to mention what effect his misfortune would have on Constance. She only has six weeks left. Do you wish her doomed?"

Only Eric had the stomach to meet her gaze, and his eyes were wide.

"I wish you would not remind me of the date," Constance murmured. "The right man will come along, Katherine. Be content to let me wait for him."

Katherine gritted her teeth. Waiting would get them all into trouble. "I do not wish you to feel pressured, love. But facts are facts. Your father, Eric's and my stepfather, was certain you needed encouragement to wed. Your incentive was his fortune, which you will lose to your cousin if you are not married by your twentieth birthday."

"That's not very far from now," Eric pointed out helpfully. "You better hurry, Constance."

She sighed. "I am trying, Eric, truly I am."

Emma patted her hand on the coverlet. "Of course

ye are, Miss Constance. Ye be so lovely, I know some handsome bloke'll snatch ye up, so he will."

As Bixby nodded, Constance offered them all a brave smile. "I pray you are right."

"I know they are right," Katherine said with equal fervor. "Just think, Constance. The perfect gentleman may appear on our doorstep tomorrow."

"Or today," Eric said with a grin and a wink to Katherine.

Katherine laid a hand on his shoulder in warning lest he give away the game with his enthusiasm. "Precisely," she said. "And with that in mind, Constance, I think you should dress in your very best."

"And which gown would that be?" Constance asked with a teasing wink. "All my clothes are lovely. You should know, for you chose most of them."

Katherine felt a pang at her manipulations. In truth, it pleased her to dress Constance in pretty clothes. Of course, with Constance's beauty, she'd have been hard-pressed to find anything that didn't look good on the girl. Constance had no way of knowing that several of the more recent acquisitions had been chosen with a far more important goal in mind than her own pleasure.

"What about that new gown I purchased for you?" Katherine asked her stepsister with a great deal more innocence than she felt.

Bixby caught her eye and nodded encouragement. "And that pretty scent you wore the other day," he said to Constance. "Like violets it was."

"Oh, *that* dress," Eric said wisely, and Katherine had to pat him again.

Constance frowned as if she had noticed their odd behavior, but she nodded. "Certainly I can do those things, if they please you."

Katherine nodded with a smile, although she knew it wasn't so much their pleasure as Lord Borin's they had in mind. Purple was his favorite color and violets his favorite flower, according to his old nurse, whom Bixby had found retired in London. If one was going to lay a trap, after all, one needed to use the proper enticement.

Of course, she didn't like thinking of it as a trap, so much as the logical solution to a problem. Katherine considered the matter as she finished up her duties that evening and settled herself into bed beside Constance. Even asleep her stepsister looked lovely. Her skin glowed in the moonlight and her breath was as soft and quiet as a newborn kitten's. Though they shared no blood, they were closer than many sisters Katherine had known. She knew from experience that her stepsister was as lovely inside as she was out. Any man should be pleased to have Constance for a bride.

Knowing that, she had not expected to have to work so hard at finding that man. Her mother and stepfather had been carried away by the influenza just before Katherine's first Season. Society called for a mourning period of no less than six months, which would have effectively canceled her Season, but she had her hands too full with sixteen-year-old Constance and five-year-old Eric to worry about what she was missing.

Sir Richard had been home recovering from his wound for over a year at that time and had assumed guardianship for them, with the help of his man, Bixby. In the beginning, her uncle had been some help to her, but it soon became clear he had no idea what to do with the three of them. His failure had only encouraged his retreat into the bottle, as far as she could tell.

Katherine had been the one to find them a house when they lost her stepfather's home to his heir, Weldon Templeman. Katherine had begged Emma, her stepfather's long-time cook, to come with them. Katherine had made sure Constance received tutoring so she could make her presentation at court and be received into society.

And now Katherine intended to see that her wonderful stepsister lived happily ever after.

She wrinkled her nose as a feather from the down comforter tickled it. At some point, she supposed, she'd have to consider what "happily ever after" meant for herself. Her twenty-second birthday would be in August. She was too old to have a Season of her own. In truth, she wasn't sure she wanted one. While she loved London with all its amusements and intrigues, she wasn't particularly enamored of parading herself in the marriage mart. The only thing she had saved for a trousseau was her mother's ruby engagement ring, a heavy, ornate piece that suited her no better than it had her gentle mother.

Once Constance was safely wed and Eric enrolled in Eton, as was his due, she thought she would be quite content to keep a small house and cultivate a select circle of friends. She might even purchase herself a harp to replace the one Constance's cousin had spitefully insisted on keeping when they left the Templeman town house.

But all that depended on Constance marrying in the next six weeks. Lord Borin was the favored candidate. Tomorrow, she would take another step toward betrothing him to her stepsister.

With the plan of attack she had in mind, the poor fellow didn't stand a chance.

Four

By the time Alex arrived at the Collins house the following afternoon, he was well pleased with himself. He rather thought the Marquis of Hastings would be proud as well of his reconnaissance, had the man known.

Of course, it hadn't been easy. He had stopped first to question his friend Kevin Whattling, who was nearly as popular among the *ton* as he was. The Corinthian was also not above a bit of gossip. Unfortunately, Whattling was on the way to a prize fight. It simply would not do to let him go alone. Only after the roar of the crowd had ceased had Alex gotten a chance to learn anything from his friend.

It seemed Whattling had already met the new Lord Templeman. The nephew of Constance Templeman's father, he had inherited the title and estates on the death of the former Lord Templeman. Constance's father had amassed his own fortune, however, which he had bequeathed to his only blood daughter. Alex found it surprising that a woman with Miss Templeman's supposed beauty and fortune had not been snatched up for marriage. Giles Sloan, friend to both him and Whattling, pointed out the obvious over dinner at

White's that night with their crony Sir Nigel Dillingham.

"She may be a beauty, but she is notoriously finicky." The rotund Sloan nodded his red head sagely. "She even refused to dance with Viscount Darton."

Sir Nigel gave one of his horselike snorts. "Demned intelligent female, if you ask me. Darton is too high in the instep."

"But is Miss Templeman any lower?" Whattling mused, poking at his beef. He glanced up at Alex with a twinkle in his blue eyes. "Something tells me she would lead even you a merry chase, Borin."

"Give me a plain girl who knows her worth," Sir Nigel muttered, "over a beauty who thinks herself a goddess."

Alex had to agree.

He also did not disagree when Sir Nigel offered to introduce him to some other gentlemen recently returned from the Peninsula. From them, Alex learned that Richard Collins had earned his knighthood after being wounded at Corunna. Collins had been part of the guard burying General Moore when hit by grapeshot. Several of Sir Nigel's acquaintances had served with Collins. All found him jovial and helpful. One, however, complained of Collins's fondness for wine and women. Alex didn't see that fondness as a weakness, for it was too much like his own life. He also couldn't see why Collins would be interested in him, unless they had somehow become rivals over the same woman. The only woman he'd pursued recently was his mistress, Lydia.

As he left White's, he almost stopped at the flat he was paying for and asked her about Sir Richard Collins, but he wasn't sure he was in the mood for her attentions. The fair Lydia had proven herself to have a rapacious appetite, which extended no farther than his purse. If Collins wanted her, Alex was ready to hand her over.

Of all he had learned, however, the most important piece of information to him was the name of the sprite at the door. Whattling had confirmed that Miss Katherine Collins was indeed the older stepsister of the lovely Miss Templeman. Her widowed mother had married the former Lord Templeman, himself a widow with child, nearly eight years ago. Miss Collins supposedly had a younger brother, but Alex had been unable to determine age. It was possible he had been the lad following him, but Alex found it difficult to believe the stepson of a lord would be allowed to wander the city in costume.

So, for all the information he had gained on the Collins household, he still wasn't certain why any of them would be interested in following him. The only way to learn more was to play out the charade and visit.

This time a butler met his knock. The fellow was dressed in a black coat and breeches. His balding head, ringed by a close-cropped fringe of silver-gray hair, was nearly as polished as his brass buttons. His narrow face was stern, reminding Alex of a master at Eton. All in all, he was as impressive a fellow as one could have wished. While Alex hadn't been expecting depravity, he found himself disappointed that the fellow didn't at least have sneaky eyes or a knowing smile.

As Alex followed him upstairs to the withdrawing room, he thought perhaps he might spot something odd about the interior of the house. Unfortunately, everywhere he looked things appeared distressingly normal. The oak banister gleamed; the walls were a cheery yellow devoid of cobwebs. Portraits of smiling ladies in jewel-toned gowns from ages past brightened the space. The corridor smelled of lemon and beeswax, testimony that a diligent housekeeper had been busy there as well.

The withdrawing room itself took up the entire back half of the upstairs, with three windows overlooking the family garden. The room was tastefully furnished with matching settee and a quartet of armchairs upholstered in soft blue velvet with gilt spindles and arms. A small fire burned in the shiny brass grate. Pastoral watercolors glowed on the green-blue walls. It was a cozy, friendly scene with which he could find no fault.

Neither could he find a single fault in Miss Templeman. She perched on the settee, hands folded in the lap of her fashionable silk gown. A prettier shade of purple he had never seen. As he stepped forward to take her hand in greeting, the scent of violets wafted over him, as soft as the welcoming light in her lovely blue eyes. He was instantly reminded of his childhood and the homey smell of violets and soap that had emanated from his Nana. He caught himself smiling at no one in particular and had to recall himself to the present.

The lady before him was no aged nurse. Golden curls framed an angelic face with upturned nose and rosebud lips. The lavender gown swelled with luscious curves. Her smile was innocent, her demeanor sweet. In fact, he was hard-pressed to think of a more perfect specimen of womanhood currently on the marriage mart. The mystery of her single state deepened.

The bigger surprise was that he found he far preferred his greeting with Miss Collins. No overwhelming sweetness there. Her impish grin was conspiratorial. Had their sexes been reversed, he thought he probably would have blushed at the gleam of appreciation in her warm brown eyes. He bowed to her, then took his seat across from her in one of the arm chairs, smoothing down the front of his navy coat.

A frown creased her brow. Before he could wonder at it, her gaze darted to the empty space beside her stepsister as if in a message. She would prefer that he sit next to Miss Templeman? What manner of woman encouraged a man to show his interests elsewhere? He perversely leaned back in the chair and crossed his booted legs.

"My uncle is unexpectedly unavailable," Miss Collins told him, but somehow she did not sound the least regretful. "Of course, you remember my stepsister Constance Templeman."

"Of course, Miss Collins," Alex replied. "Miss Templeman, your servant."

He was rewarded to see Miss Collins start. She apparently hadn't thought he could learn her name. He wasn't sure why her surprise pleased him. Her grin quickly returned, as if she were delighted to discover that he was clever. He ought to be insulted, but instead he grinned back.

"How nice to see you again, Lord Borin," Miss Templeman said, her voice soft and melodious, as perfect as the rest of her. "You will remember that we met at Lady Monk's musicale last Season."

In truth, he had forgotten. Now that she mentioned it, however, he remembered seeing her there. She had been in the company of a large ponderous fellow. He somehow didn't think it was Sir Richard. It must have been the new Lord Templeman. Alex nodded politely. "Yes, I remember. Do you enjoy music, Miss Templeman?"

It was the most innocent of conversations, designed to put them at their ease. He was confident he could maneuver the discussion around to something more useful. Unfortunately, Miss Templeman was not particularly helpful.

"I love music," she replied fervently, though her smile was sad. "I must admit, however, that hearing it makes me regret that I never learned an instrument."

"You missed nothing," Miss Collins put in quickly. "My mother had me take lessons on the harp for ten years and my thumb still persists in pointing upward when I hold out my hands. Be thankful you have such a sweet singing voice."

A lovely voice was another accomplishment he should have expected from the beautiful Miss Templeman. He had a harder time envisioning Miss Collins at the harp. She looked far too devilish to play such an angelic instrument.

Her stepsister blushed becomingly. "Thank you, Katherine, but you know I do not like such attention as singing alone gives me. I quite prefer our duets."

Now that was something he'd like to see. "I imagine the two of you are delightful together. Perhaps you might favor me."

Miss Templeman immediately demurred, blush deepening. Miss Collins merely smiled. He watched her lips curling in satisfaction and wondered if they were as soft as they looked. Before he could chide himself for such wayward thoughts, her gaze darted once more to her stepsister, drawing his eyes there instead. Confound the woman! Why did she persist in throwing Miss Templeman at his head?

"Did you have a particular purpose in calling on Sir Richard today?" her stepsister asked. "Perhaps we might be of assistance."

The question recalled him to his duty. He was here for information, after all. "I understand we may have mutual friends in the same regiment," he offered. "Has he perchance been trying to make my acquaintance?"

Miss Templeman frowned. Miss Collins's eyes narrowed as if she were trying to see through the holes in his story.

"We have heard nothing in that regard," she answered for both of them. "But surely you are far too busy to spend time reminiscing with old soldiers. Did I not hear you recently purchased an impressive mount, my lord? The foal of an Ascot winner, I believe?"

Before Alex knew it, he was prosing on about his stables, his horses, and their upcoming races. Miss Templeman was a rapt audience, but he gradually became aware that Miss Collins steadfastly refused to join the conversation unless it was to subtly point out her stepsister's finer characteristics. Try as he might, Alex could not get them to discuss their guardian or anything else of import.

And he quickly found himself growing bored. The only thing he had managed to learn was that Miss Templeman was not the snob Giles Sloan had suggested. Indeed, she was rather cloyingly sweet. He found he far preferred the spice of the older stepsister.

He would have to try Sir Richard directly if he wanted answers. That had been his intention all along, but Miss Collins was too good at diverting his attention, in more ways than one. He was about to find an excuse to take his leave when the butler hurried in to whisper in Miss Collins's ear. She immediately jumped to her feet, forcing Alex to rise as well.

"A small problem downstairs," she explained. "If you will excuse me a moment." She flew from the room. The butler took up sentinel at the door.

Alex would have thought it a ploy to get him alone with Miss Templeman, except the girl seemed oblivious to the fact. Her conversation was no more pointed than before. In fact, without Miss Collins's guiding influence, it seemed sadly lacking. Besides, with the butler in the background Miss Templeman could hardly claim to be compromised. Before he could wonder further, Miss Collins returned with a rotund older gentleman at her heels. That she was less than pleased by the fact was evident in the tight set of her mouth.

Alex rose again as she made the introductions. "Viscount Borin, may I present Weldon, Lord Templeman."

"Miss Templeman's cousin," the man added with a heavy wheeze. He stuck out a meaty hand, which Alex accepted. "Good to meet you, Borin. I heard you had taken to visiting. It is best that we talk before matters go any further."

Alex frowned. How did the man know he had been visiting? Had the Collinses mentioned it somehow? He peered closer at the fellow, noting the narrowed blue eyes and the stubborn chin. Suspicion might have been forgiven. What was impossible to overlook, however, were the dabs of congealed gravy dotting the fellow's rumpled cravat and dusty brown coat and trousers.

Miss Collins saved Alex from an ungentlemanly response. "This is only Lord Borin's second visit," she pointed out to Templeman. "And he is here to see Sir Richard."

"Oh, yes, of course," Lord Templeman replied with a sly wink at Alex. "And my lovely cousin has nothing to do with it."

Alex raised his quizzing glass and impaled the overly bold Templeman through it. The mushroom merely frowned slightly, heavy brown brows gathering over his short nose. Alex let the glass fall in dismissal and turned to Miss Templeman.

"I believe I have overstayed my welcome, Miss Templeman."

"Got an appointment, have you?" Templeman all but sneered as his cousin sighed in obvious disappointment that Alex would leave. "One more willing, eh?"

Alex stared at him. Again the creature refused to quail. Had the fellow no idea how insulting his conversation was to the ladies? Both were tinged pink. By the way Miss Templeman lowered her gaze to the floral carpet, it was obvious that she was acutely embarrassed. By the way Miss Collins glared at Templeman, she was furious. The man was either a complete blockhead or an entire rudesby or both.

"Miss Collins," Alex said, "I regret I must take my leave. Do give my regards to your uncle."

Her shoulders sagged as if in defeat. "Of course, my lord. Let me see you out."

Templeman bowed with such a self-satisfied smile that Alex had to clamp his mouth shut to keep from giving the fellow a well-deserved set down. He pitied Miss Templeman to the core. He also thought he understood why the poor girl was unwed. Who'd want that in the family? He followed Miss Collins from the room.

They had not reached the stairs before she stopped him. "Please do not let Lord Templeman deter you, my lord. I know Constance would be delighted to have you call again."

"Your welcome is too kind," Alex replied firmly, "but as I said, I am calling on your uncle. Will he be available tomorrow, do you know?"

"Perhaps," she said slowly, and Alex was certain she was hedging. "If you could give me a time for your visit, I might contrive to make him available."

Now what did that mean? His imagination easily conjured up Collins hiding in some dark underworld lair, surrounded by knife-toting, rum-swilling henchmen, while his niece pleaded for a moment of his time. The vision popped as quickly as it had formed. Very likely the fellow did nothing more heinous with his time than disappear to his club to reminisce with his cronies. Alex was chasing a phantom.

"Do not trouble yourself," he told her. "I will try another avenue to answer my questions. I would not want anyone to read more into these visits than I intended. Lord Templeman appears to think an offer is imminent."

She grimaced. "Lord Templeman always thinks an offer is imminent. He is simply insistent on doing his duty toward his family."

"If that is the case," Alex replied thoughtfully, "why doesn't Miss Templeman live with him?"

"He is a bachelor. It would be unseemly."

The excuse was plausible, but the way she said it made him wonder whether it was the only reason. Was it Sir Richard or Lord Templeman who had something to hide?

She laid a hand on his arm, a gentle touch. Glancing down, he met her gaze. The gray of her eyes was as cool and soft as mist rising on a lake.

"Please, my lord?" she murmured. "Please call again soon. I am certain my uncle will be up to receiving you in a day or two."

Why not? something inside him urged. He might yet learn a thing or two. There were worse ways to spend his time. Alex nodded. "Very well, Miss Collins," he agreed. "I shall call again in a few days."

He could not resist bringing her dainty hand to his lips and pressing a kiss against the back. He could feel the tremor up her arm.

What surprised him was the answering quiver inside him.

Five

Katherine closed the door with a heartfelt sigh. Things were not going as she'd planned. Lord Borin had obviously noticed their intentions and made inquiries. How else could he have come by her name? She felt rather pleased that he would take the trouble to learn it. He was brighter than she'd expected based on the information they had gathered. Most of the gentlemen she had met who preferred to pass their time gaming and racing were not intellectual giants. Of course, she probably should have expected more intelligence after his nurse had boasted of the marks he'd received at Eton.

She also hadn't counted on interference from Lord Templeman quite so quickly. How had he known Lord Borin had called previously? Was the old codger spying on them? She hadn't thought him that cunning. Indeed, every gambit her stepsister's cousin tried was pathetically obvious.

Like his attempt to scare away Lord Borin.

Katherine sighed again as she climbed the stairs for the withdrawing room. As she had expected, she found Constance nearly in tears. She hurried to take a seat beside her stepsister.

"I tell you this for your well-being," Templeman

was saying in his usual pompous manner, one plump hand smoothing back his mane of graying hair. "You must have a care for your reputation. Gentlemen have an aversion to marrying a woman who is thought unchaste."

As Constance bravely sucked on her lower lip, Katherine nearly choked. "No one would dare imply Constance less than a lady," she informed Lord Templeman. "Emma, Bixby, or I attend her every minute a gentleman visits. She is always chaperoned when she goes out."

Lord Templeman leaned back with an audible creak of his corset. "One can never be too careful. Just associating with someone like Borin might be enough to darken her name."

Constance's limpid eyes widened.

Katherine frowned. "What do you mean? We have heard no bad report of Lord Borin."

"Well, certainly, *you* wouldn't," Templeman replied with a smug smile. "These are tales passed among gentlemen, if you take my meaning."

"I thought a real gentleman never boasted of his conquests," Katherine countered, remembering something she had heard Sir Richard tell Eric when he had asked about a certain lady.

"And a lady never admits to understanding the reference," Templeman sneered. "But perhaps I berate the wrong person in Constance. Where is your guardian, Sir Richard? Why isn't he here protecting her?"

"Sir Richard is unwell," Katherine replied, hoping he would not ask the nature of the illness. Bixby had reported that two brandy bottles had been found in her uncle's study last night before he was carried off to bed. She supposed she should be thankful he didn't overdose himself with laudanum or morphine instead.

"Ah, unwell. Again." Templeman shook his head.

"What a topsy-turvy household you have, to be sure. I begin to think I should remove my cousin, for her own good."

Constance gasped, and Katherine quickly covered her stepsister's hands with one of her own. "Now, Lord Templeman," she scolded, "what would the gossips say, a handsome bachelor such as yourself sharing his lodging with a young lady?"

She nearly gagged on the sentiment, but it worked its charm as she had known it would. Templeman sat straighter, forcing another creak from the vicinity of his body, and preened. "Yes, well, there is that, I suppose. Still in all, we must do our best for Miss Constance."

"And in that vein," Katherine said, seizing her advantage, "I still do not see why you object to Lord Borin. He is more handsome and wealthy than most of Constance's suitors."

"He seems quite charming," Constance put in wistfully.

Katherine was encouraged by the tone. It was obvious, however, that it only discouraged Lord Templeman. "Well, if I must spell it out for you," he blustered, "he is a cad. If you want proof, you have only to look at the string of mistresses he's kept, the latest of which is Lydia Montgomery, the actress at Drury Lane."

Constance paled at the revelation. Katherine merely pursed her lips in thought. She would have liked to dismiss the tale as gossip, but the reference was too specific. Of course, Lord Templeman could not know that she had ways of confirming his information.

"I had heard," she said carefully, "that some men who dally are easily reformed by marriage."

"Lady Janice Willstencraft says that reformed rakes make the best husbands," Constance agreed.

Katherine wasn't certain she'd trust the green-eyed

Lady Janice on the definition of a good husband. It was known she had already refused six completely eligible suitors of her own. Katherine could only hope her stepsister hadn't taken any other advice from the volatile young debutante.

"What balderdash," Lord Templeman replied with an ill-bred snort. "Once a dallier, always a dallier, I say. Do you wish your stepsister wed to a reprobate, Miss Collins?"

"A reprobate?" Constance cried.

"Lord Borin," Katherine said hotly, "is no reprobate. He earned credible marks at Eton, his estate is well managed, and his servants find him even handed and even tempered. He has never been caught cheating at cards. When he owes a debt, he pays it promptly. He even donates to worthy charities, for pity's sake!"

"I see he has been busy bragging," Lord Templeman sneered. "Do you believe everything you are told, Miss Collins?"

"Only when it comes from a reputable source, Lord Templeman."

His eyes narrowed as his face reddened. He heaved his considerable bulk out of the chair. The intimidating movement was spoiled by yet another creak. As Katherine forced herself to smile instead of laugh at him, he wagged a finger in her face. "You have been warned, miss. Borin is a loose fish, and I will not countenance him for Constance."

Katherine rose as well. She stood in front of him, head raised to meet his angry gaze. "You did not countenance any of her suitors so far. However, I have no doubt Sir Richard will see Lord Borin's interest in a different light. You will remember, sir, that it is *his* decision whom my stepsister marries."

"No," Constance said. The quiet determination in her voice drew Katherine's gaze to her, and she noticed

Lord Templeman had been similarly affected. For once, Constance did not flinch when she found herself the center of attention. "It is my decision whom I marry," she told them. "I did not love either of the gentlemen who offered, and so I asked Sir Richard to refuse them. It remains to be seen whether I shall love Lord Borin."

Templeman glanced at Katherine in triumph, then reached over to pat Constance's shoulder. "You are a good girl, Cousin. I know I can count on you to do what is right, unlike some others."

"Oh, my," Katherine sang out in pure spite, "look at the time! We have detained you, my lord. Bixby, show Lord Templeman to the door immediately."

Templeman did not fight her, merely chuckling as he bowed and left the room.

Katherine sank onto the settee beside her stepsister. "Whatever possessed you to agree with him, Constance?"

She smiled sadly. "Whatever possessed you to disagree? You know you cannot win against him. My cousin is a potent force."

"At least in his own mind," Katherine grumbled. "You cannot give in to him, Constance. Can you not see he is after your fortune? If he can keep you from marrying for another six weeks, you will lose everything."

"I know," Constance replied with a sigh. "But I cannot bring myself to marry without love. It is as if I am buying a husband. I could not respect a man who would marry me under such circumstances."

Katherine sighed as well, reaching out to take her hands. "But dearest, you are constantly surrounded by suitors when we go out, and any number of them would be willing to brave your cousin's defenses if you would encourage them. Has none of them touched your heart?"

"None," she confided, withdrawing from the touch. "I find them rather tiresome."

"What of Kevin Whattling, who danced with you at Lady Lorton's party?" Katherine challenged. "You cannot say he isn't handsome."

"He is quite handsome," Constance agreed. "But his hands sweat. I swear I could feel them through his gloves and mine."

"The Marquis DeGuis, then. Every lady in London is said to be swooning."

"He is much too cool for my liking. Just having him look down his nose when he greeted me was enough to make me wish myself elsewhere."

"And Everett Wardman? I thought his conversation most animated after services last Sunday."

"He drinks to excess. I have experience enough of that to know how sadly it can end."

"Sir Richard cannot help himself," Katherine protested loyally. When Constance merely eyed her, blue eyes solemn, she sighed. "Oh, very well. I cannot argue that having a sot for a husband would be a miserable existence. But there are others more sober, with a cheery smile and dry palms. I will not allow you to dismiss them so easily."

Constance smiled. "I think you favor Lord Borin."

Katherine swallowed. "I am sure I do not know what you mean."

"You were quite vocal in your defense of him before my cousin. I thank you for that. I agree he is an amiable man, and handsome enough for any girl. However, I noticed the way your eyes lit when he entered the room. I have never seen you smile so. Are you certain you would not like him to pursue you instead?"

Katherine hopped to her feet. "Me? I am not the one ready to give away her fortune to a dastard."

"If it does not trouble me," Constance said, gazing

up at her with a slight frown of her golden brows, "why should it trouble you?"

Why indeed? She felt selfish just considering the answer. Sir Richard had a small pension, and her mother and father had left them a little. Even combined the money was not enough to keep renting this house they had taken when her stepfather died. Constance's cousin had made no secret that he would prefer to see Eric in the military and Katherine in the workhouse, if he had his way about matters. She did not think it would come to that, but they would not be able to keep living this way if Constance lost her fortune.

She tried not to spend her stepsister's money on fripperies. She remade her mother's dresses and helped Sir Richard tutor Eric to save funds. They seldom entertained; Constance's popularity was sufficient to ensure they never lacked for invitations elsewhere. They kept no servants other than the ever-loyal Bixby and Emma. All that would change if Constance became as poor as they were. She could not put that burden on her stepsister.

Some of what she was feeling must have showed on her face, for Constance's frown deepened. "What is it, Katherine? Does the loss of my fortune affect you?"

"It does not signify," she replied, returning to her seat. "The most important thing is and shall be your happiness. If none of these gentlemen fits the bill, we will simply have to find another. For the moment, let us concentrate on Lord Borin."

Constance agreed, countenance once more sunny. Katherine sent her upstairs to prepare for her afternoon of calling on her fashionable friends. As she often did, Constance begged her to join them.

"You keep yourself too much in the shade," her stepsister chided. "You cannot spend all your time managing this house. Leave something for Emma and come with me."

Katherine demurred. She would not deny Emma's considerable abilities, but she could not leave their cook and housekeeper to bear the work alone. Besides, Katherine had another idea entirely of how she wanted to spend her time today. Once her stepsister was out of the house with Emma as chaperon, she grabbed Bixby from his duties.

"The War Office," she ordered. "I'll get Eric."

They met a few moments later across from the schoolroom, in a bedchamber that had once housed the governess for the former tenants. Before the Season had started, Katherine had appropriated it for her own use. Now the white plaster walls were covered with pieces of paper nailed in place. On them were noted every bit of information they had been able to learn about Lord Borin. They had neatly categorized the information as "likes," "dislikes," "daily routine," and "to be verified." Thanks to Bixby and Eric, the last category had been emptied, until now.

While Eric curled up on the braided rug before the small hearth and Bixby seated himself on a high-backed chair they had purloined from the kitchen, Katherine proceeded to write down the newest bit of information, tacking it determinedly in place.

"Lord Templeman says Borin has a mistress," she declared.

Bixby grimaced. "We should have caught that. I knew you should have let me follow him more often at night."

"Sir Richard would have noticed your absence from the dinner table. And I was too often out with Constance." She shook her head. "We will simply have to verify it."

"What's a mistress?" Eric piped up.

Katherine felt herself blushing, but Bixby supplied the answer. "A woman who acts like a wife but isn't one."

"Is that bad?" Eric asked with a frown, absently scratching his arm through his brown wool jacket.

"For Lord Borin, no," Katherine answered. "For our purposes, yes. If he already has something like a wife, he may not be interested in getting himself a real one."

"So what do we do?"

"I say we continue as we have," Bixby said. "Any man who realizes how sweet Miss Constance is would be happy to throw off a mistress for her."

"Ordinarily, I would agree," Katherine replied, while Eric looked thoughtful. "But we all know how Constance vacillates. I do not believe she has decided whether she is truly interested in Lord Borin."

"Isn't that just like a girl?" Eric muttered.

Katherine glared at him. "Mind your mouth, young sir. I refuse to believe an eight-year-old knows how girls do or do not behave, particularly after having me for a sister."

"Now, Miss Katherine," Bixby chided, "you're not so different a young miss. You like pretty clothes well enough."

Katherine couldn't help gazing down at her navy bombazine. "Well, I did when I was younger. But that is neither here nor there. I still say Lord Borin is our best candidate. We agreed on that after looking over the prospects carefully before the Season began." She waved a hand at the pieces of paper surrounding them. "Look at this information and tell me he isn't perfect."

Bixby glanced about. "It certainly seemed that way, Miss Katherine. He was stable, well heeled, and well liked. I don't see how we failed."

"We cannot fail. She simply has to see more of him. To do that, we need his full attention. Bixby?"

Her butler stood at attention. "Miss?"

"See what you can learn about Lydia Montgomery, the actress. What are her interests, her tastes, her financial status? Are there other gentlemen besides Lord Borin interested in her?"

"Aye, Colonel," he agreed with a wink and a salute.

"What about me?" Eric asked, hopping to his feet as well. "You aren't going to make me go back to my studies, are you?"

"You will be pleased you put in time on your studies when you are admitted to Eton," she reminded him.

He made a face. "So you insist. I think you just like ordering me around. Why can't I follow Lord Borin some more?"

"Because he's seen you," she replied with a shake of her head. "Best you keep out of his way just as you did today." His elfin face puckered, and she smiled. "But I still need you. Go over our information carefully. See if you can find any discrepancies. If we are to succeed in our objective of capturing Lord Borin's heart, we need to know everything about him. We have little time. There must be more than one way to catch a husband."

Six

Lord Templeman left the Collins house well satisfied. He had scared off Borin, at least for the moment, and made his cousin think twice about seeing him again. He had even needled the odious Miss Collins in the process. It only took the short drive home, however, for the doubts to set in.

He stomped into the town house he had inherited from his uncle and shoved his hat and gloves at the trembling manservant. The satin-hung walls echoed as he shouted for his tea. He stalked across the hall to the study and threw himself into the armchair. The puff of dust that rose as he did so only reminded him that his second housekeeper in a month had quit that morning.

Sinking deeper into the richly upholstered chair, he felt his face settle into a scowl. So close! Less than six more weeks and the fortune would be his. All he had to do was discourage any young men and keep the rumors alive about Constance's snobbery. It had caused him a little trouble to spread them to begin with, but fanning the flames was all too easy. She was so lovely that most were quite willing to believe she had some hidden flaw. And most of the young men who were not daunted by the rumors were usually easily daunted by him.

Borin, however, might be more difficult. He rubbed his lips back and forth against each other as he thought. Borin was such a perfect candidate that the only way to disparage him was to dredge up the fellow's mistress. Not a particularly heinous crime. Most fellows with any income kept a ladybird on the side. He had two at the moment, biddable tarts both. Still, a true lady should be scandalized by such habits.

Constance, of course, had been just that. That Collins chit, unfortunately, had no sense of her proper place. Meddlesome witch. How he'd like to see her settled picking hemp in the poorhouse. That would mend her ways. She seemed to think herself his better, and him with the title! She'd be singing another tune when he took that fortune away from her.

If he could take the fortune. This situation with Borin would bear scrutiny. He reached out and yanked the bellpull to summon his man. A few notes delivered to the right people should do the trick. Amazing how many were willing to do him a favor when they realized he would shortly be coming into a fortune. He already had someone watching the Collins house for him. It would take little to have them watch Borin as well. He'd learned a few tricks before ascending to the title on the death of his far-more-proper uncle. If Lord Borin continued to call, he could easily take more drastic measures. He smiled just thinking of them.

Alexander Wescott, Viscount Borin, might be the consummate gentleman with his golden looks and fashionable coats, but he would do well not to trouble himself with the Collins family, or Weldon, Lord Templeman.

* * *

Fortunately for Alex, the recipients of Lord Templeman's notes could not take action immediately. Indeed, had Templeman known how Alex spent the rest of the afternoon and the next day, he would have had apoplexy. Alex visited any number of friends and relatives and discretely probed their knowledge of one Weldon, Lord Templeman. To Alex's surprise, he found few people who knew him well. Those who knew him at all were not particularly strong in their praise.

"Hasn't been voted membership at White's, if you noticed," Sloan observed.

"Loose fish," Sir Nigel proclaimed. "Cheats at cards. Don't care whether the fellow inherited the title. That was one barony that would have been better off going into abeyance, if you take my meaning."

On a chance during one of his boxing workouts, he asked some of the rougher types who frequented Gentleman Jackson's. Most knew nothing of the man, but one fellow was loud in his complaints, calling Templeman a devil's spawn. Alex's curiosity was sufficient that he decided to hire a Bow Street Runner to look into the matter. The wiry gentleman in the red waistcoat promised to be circumspect and to provide Alex with a report on his progress in a few days.

Just to be on the safe side, he asked the fellow to learn what he could of the Collinses as well. Alex doubted he'd learn anything of note, but he wanted to be thorough in his investigation. He felt certain Templeman would be his culprit. The boy Alex had followed a few days ago had likely belonged to Templeman and the creature was using the lad to spy on his cousin. How else would he know precisely when Alex was calling? The question remained—why go to such lengths?

In the interest of thoroughness, he assured himself, he simply had to call on the Collinses again. Besides, he had promised as much to Miss Collins. His growing attraction to her, of course, had nothing to do with the decision. Neither did it have anything to do with the inordinate amount of time it took him to dress for their next meeting. He finally chose a bottle-green coat over a silk waistcoat of jade and chamois trousers. He arrived at the door at precisely three the next day.

As before, the butler showed him to the withdrawing room, where Miss Collins and her stepsister joined him shortly. Both were all smiles, and he complimented them on their fine looks. Miss Collins looked pleased, even though the amusement in her expressive gray eyes told him she disagreed with him that her spruce gown was as charming as he made it out to be. Miss Templeman blushed charmingly. She obviously knew that the blue cotton gown matched her eyes. Neither bothered to mention their absent guardian. He decided he would continue the charade.

"And how is Sir Richard this afternoon?" he asked politely.

They exchanged glances before his sprite answered, "Better, thank you. I expect him to join us shortly."

That was news. A part of him had begun to wonder whether the fellow had decamped for distant shores. "Excellent," he replied. "And I trust all is well with you both?"

"We are fine, my lord," Miss Templeman answered. "And you?"

"Never better."

They lapsed into silence, and he watched as Miss Collins's gaze darted between his face and her stepsister's. Was she still trying to gauge his interest? The game was becoming tiresome. But if he played it as well, he might gain something for his trouble.

"I know you must be busy, Miss Templeman," he said, "this being the Season and all. I feel I should not impose on your time." They both started to demur, and he hurried quickly on. "I therefore wondered, Miss Collins, whether *you* might accompany me on a drive through Hyde Park tomorrow."

She blinked, then smiled. "Why certainly, Lord Borin. I would be delighted to chaperon you and Constance."

He gritted his teeth. She could not have misunderstood him. Her stepsister even realized the error.

"No, dear," she said, "I believe Lord Borin is inviting you."

"No, he isn't," Miss Collins snapped, then turned to him sternly. "You would not do such a thing, my lord. You would invite Constance. And I am certain she would be delighted to join you."

Just once he wished he didn't feel the necessity to act the gentleman. "Of course, Miss Collins. Miss Templeman, I would be honored to drive with you."

"You are too kind, my lord," she murmured, eyes downcast.

"Say four, then?" her stepsister put in. "I shall see that she is ready for you."

She made it sound like her stepsister was a refurbished carriage, or a Covent Garden tart. He glanced at Miss Templeman, but her eyes were still on the toes of her dainty white slippers. He glanced at his sprite and found her positively glaring at him. Perhaps it would be wiser to take his leave. Before he could do so, she hopped to her feet.

"I do not know what is keeping Sir Richard," she exclaimed. "Let me fetch him for you." She darted past the butler and ran from the room. Watching her, Alex let a sigh escape. He turned to catch Miss Templeman eyeing him.

"You do not fool me, my lord," she said firmly.

Alex widened his eyes, trying to look innocent.

"Fool you, Miss Templeman? Why should I want to fool you?"

"You wanted to drive with Katherine," she replied.

He relaxed. For a moment he had thought she knew his true purpose in coming. Unfortunately, when her stepsister was around, even he found himself forgetting. He inclined his head. "Forgive me, Miss Templeman. I am, of course, delighted to have you both join me."

She smiled. "And you are too much the gentleman to say if you thought otherwise. I shall try to see you are rewarded for your gallantry."

He raised a brow, wondering exactly what reward she meant. His gaze was drawn to her smiling mouth, but his mind readily substituted the fuller lips of her stepsister. He shook his head to clear the thought as much as to refuse her praise. Before he could speak, however, Sir Richard Collins entered.

Alex made his acquaintance eagerly, once more ready to find something out of the ordinary. Unfortunately, Sir Richard looked nothing like a villain. He was tall, with dark auburn hair that waved about his ears, and a warm gaze that reminded Alex of Miss Collins. There, however, the resemblance ended. Though Collins's smile was welcoming, his eyes were sunken in a face gone pale and slack. Remembering the stories of the man's bravery under fire, Alex wondered whether the wound still caused him to suffer. He tended to shift frequently in the chair. The movement could have been caused by discomfort from his wound, or too much energy. An occasional grimace, quickly hidden, told Alex that it was his leg that pained him.

He had hoped Miss Collins might join them but was disappointed to find she did not return. Instead, Miss Templeman excused herself and left the two men alone. They conversed for a time, learning that they did indeed share several friends in the military. They also shared the opinion that the war must be ended sooner rather than later. Alex slipped in a few questions of a more probing nature but saw nothing that indicated that Sir Richard was evading him. He felt sufficiently comfortable, in fact, to be forthright with the fellow.

"Your wards seem to suspect that I came here courting," he confessed. "I said I came to meet you. However, I must confide another motive."

"Oh?" Sir Richard prompted.

"I do not agree with you that swift military action alone can turn the tide of this war. There is another battle being waged, across the countryside and in our drawing rooms, a battle of wits."

"You speak of espionage," Sir Richard mused. "Counterintelligence. Isn't that the province of Calhoun and his men?"

"For battle reconnaissance, certainly, but who infiltrates the ranks of French aristocrats to unearth Napoleon's plans? Who prevents our enemies from gaining similar access to our plans?"

His brow cleared. "Ah, Lord Hastings's Service."

"Precisely. It is my ambition to join them. To do so, I must solve a mystery."

"The spy among the *ton?*"

"You know about that?" Alex shifted in his seat, trying to withhold suspicion.

"I am not completely absent from society," Sir Richard informed him. "I heard the rumor some time ago. Surely you cannot think it holds water."

"I did not, at first. But Lord Hastings has been more evident at a number of parties lately."

Sir Richard nodded thoughtfully. "Do you have a suspect then?"

"No, worst luck. And I do not have leave to investigate the matter. However, I have a mystery that may well be connected."

"I shall help in any way I can." He grimaced suddenly. "As long as it does not involve walking."

"I understand. And I do not believe walking is required." Alex glanced over his shoulder, noting with satisfaction that the butler had busied himself elsewhere. Nonetheless, he lowered his voice. "I am being followed. I must learn by whom and for what purpose. I nearly caught the boy the last time he tried it, but he disappeared, into this house."

Collins frowned. "Here? You are certain of that?"

"Positive. He slipped into your kitchen two days ago, as if he were well familiar with it. I can only conclude by the fact that he was not forcefully evicted that your staff were equally familiar with him. Do you know who he could be? Do you have a lad on staff?"

"No," he replied, rubbing his nose with a finger. "At least, not that I am aware of. My niece Katherine makes the household arrangements. Can you describe this boy, my lord?"

"Perhaps four feet tall, slender." Alex realized with a pang just how little he'd seen. "His hair was obscured by a cap, but it could have been auburn. His face was smudged with soot. I didn't get more than a glimpse of a gamin grin."

"Pity." He shook his head. "Let me speak to my niece and the staff. Perhaps they can tell us more. If I learn anything, I shall send word. You have a house in town?"

Alex gave him the address and rose to leave. He would have liked to question the staff right then, but he respected Collins's right to do so privately. He would have liked more to have another word with Collins's sprightly niece, but he caught no sight of her as the butler reappeared to lead him to the door. He would have to be content with the knowledge that she would drive with him on the morrow.

Richard limped down the corridor for his study. Bixby hadn't restocked the liquor, he noted, but for once he didn't mind. The puzzle the young lord had handed him would require a keen mind to solve. He barely noted the familiar ache in his thigh as he hobbled to the desk beside the front window.

So, a young lad had been shadowing Lord Borin. The description could easily match his nephew Eric, and certainly the scamp would have welcomed the adventure. But he saw no reason for Eric to choose Lord Borin as his target. If the culprit was his nephew, someone had clearly put him up to it.

There were several people who might make such a request other than himself. But Eric would never obey an order from Lord Templeman, and neither Constance nor Emma would dare give such an order to begin with. Bixby was thoroughly capable of masterminding the affair. He was the only person in the household who knew that Richard had always had two supervisors during his time in the military. One was General Moore, to whom he had been an attaché. The other was Lord Hastings. Bixby had often been the go-between. When Richard had been wounded that dark day in Spain, Bixby had joined him in retirement. They were two of a kind, or had been until recently. But he could see no reason for Bix to want to learn more about Lord Borin.

No, he was clearly seeing the work of the little Colonel.

Katherine's stepfather had given her that name, but Richard had seen at once that it was perfect for her. From the moment she could talk, she had directed those around her. He often thought her need to control her world had started when her father, his brother, had died, another casualty of war. Though as sweet tempered as Constance, his sister-in-law Eudora had been no match for raising a girl and a boy still a babe in arms. Katherine had become the voice of logic in that household.

The former Lord Templeman had been one of the few who could harness her skills. He'd given her opportunities to help him manage his estates and his household. A shame all that had gone to Constance's cousin on the man's death. Left with only two servants and her immediate family, Katherine's talents were largely wasted.

So, perhaps she'd decided to put them to greater use. He knew she would never do anything nefarious or criminal. But neither could he conceive of a logical reason for her to wish to investigate Lord Borin. She couldn't be motivated by revenge. Borin might have tried to trifle with her affections, but Katherine wouldn't have allowed it.

No, something else was going on, and it looked as if he was the only one who could learn what. He'd keep an eye on both Katherine and Eric over the next few days and see what he could see.

Perhaps there was use in this old crippled warrior after all.

Seven

"Report," Katherine ordered the following morning in their War Office. "Bixby?"

"Miss Lydia Montgomery is indeed connected to Lord Borin," her butler replied, standing straight before the ladder-back chair. "However, my sources tell me his lordship grows tired of the arrangement."

She felt a ripple of pleasure. Perhaps she had had an effect on him after all. Or rather, Constance had. "Interesting," she allowed. "Anything special about Miss Montgomery we can use to encourage the dissolution?"

"She prefers red roses, Irish whiskey, and Indian rubies."

Katherine tapped a quill against her chin. "Somehow I doubt the first two will be enough to convince her to let Lord Borin go. The only ruby we have is Mother's ring. Would Miss Montgomery accept that as a bribe?"

Bixby's face fell. "Oh, Miss Katherine, no! You wouldn't give away your mother's engagement ring to someone like Miss Montgomery."

"Think, Bixby," she snapped. "I shall never use it. With any luck, Eric will make his fortune and buy a far better token for his bride."

Eric nodded. "When I become a privateer, I'll have treasure enough to pick from."

Katherine smiled at him as he stood proudly in his worn brown suit. Returning her gaze to Bixby, she found him regarding her with such sympathy in his deep-set eyes that she almost relented. But their future was too important to risk on silly sentimentality over a gold-bound stone. "I shall be fine, Bix," she assured him. "The question is, would Mother's ring do the trick?"

"It might," he allowed. "If we could ensure another gentleman taking his lordship's place in her affections immediately."

"See what you can do," Katherine advised, "and report back to me this evening. Eric?"

Her brother snapped to attention. "Ma'am! I reviewed his lordship's information. I have only one change to report. He visited the War Office, the real one in Whitehall, again the day I led him here." He sagged and quirked a regretful grin. "I forgot to note it sooner."

Katherine frowned. "The War Office? That is twice since the Season started. Is he contemplating buying a commission?"

Eric shook his head. "He didn't go in the door where they take the other recruits. He went in a tradesman's entrance."

Bixby stiffened, and Katherine eyed him with a frown.

"Was it a small archway off the King's Mews in Whitehall?" he asked Eric sharply. "Was there an officer on guard by the arch?"

Eric nodded. "That's right. A fancy-jacketed captain."

"What does it mean, Bix?" Katherine probed. "Whom do you suspect?"

Bixby scratched his chin casually, but he avoided her gaze. "Seems to me that I heard that was the private entrance to the Marquis of Hastings's office."

"The Secret Service?" Katherine felt a chill run up her spine.

Eric snorted. "Not much of a secret if even old Bixby knows about it."

Bixby affixed him with a sharp blue glare. "Don't disparage what you don't understand, whippersnapper. All of London may know that the Marquis of Hastings recruits the aristocracy into his service, but no one really knows who actually works for him, and under what circumstances. If Lord Borin is one of his, we should stop surveillance before we get caught."

"Agreed," Katherine replied. "It sounds as if we know enough about Lord Borin, in any event. Besides, if his lordship is so desperate for entertainment that he would consider joining the war effort, we owe it to him to see him safely wed instead. I should not like to see him killed or wounded like Father and Sir Richard."

They disbanded then, but as she went about her other duties that morning, she couldn't seem to remove from her mind the image of Lord Borin wounded. She had had more than enough experience with the wages of war. She didn't remember much about her own father. As an officer under General Moore, he had been away fighting much of her life. He had been killed several years before Sir Richard had been wounded.

She remembered far more about Jonathan, the former Lord Templeman, who had been her stepfather. A gentle man with a kind heart and a keen sense of appreciation for the talents of others, he had made her feel as if she could accomplish anything. She had very nearly had to do just that to keep their family together since he and her mother had died.

And then there was Sir Richard. Unlike her father, he frequently managed time to return to England. She remembered him visiting often as she was growing up. There was always a smile on his face and laughter in his eyes. He had never been too busy to take tea with her, to set her up in front of him on his fine mount, to make faces at her while she practiced her harp. How he had changed after his wound. She rarely saw a smile now. And he could barely find time to help Eric with his lessons, let alone assist her in managing their affairs. She could not let such a fate await Lord Borin.

Her plan rationalized, she waited for his arrival that afternoon. She had already determined how she would slip away before he left with Constance, forcing them to drive alone. Once Constance felt the full effect of his charm, she was sure, her stepsister would be lost. Lord Borin would be just as lost. She'd seen few men who could resist Constance's dewy beauty, at least until Lord Templeman bullied them away.

"Psst, Miss Katherine," Bixby hissed from the entry. "He just drove up."

"And in a fine high-perch phaeton, too," Eric called, one eye to the narrow window beside the door. "Look at that pair of blacks! If Constance doesn't want a ride, may I go?"

"You," Katherine said firmly, pulling him back and giving him a hug, "are supposed to remain out of sight. Now scat, and tell Constance to hurry."

But Constance didn't hurry, and Katherine was forced to receive the viscount alone while Bixby went to fetch the girl.

"I cannot think what could be keeping her," Katherine assured him, noting with approval his immaculately tailored deep blue coat and lighter blue trousers. "Constance is usually so punctual."

"Perhaps she decided a drive was not quite the thing

today," he replied with a winning smile that lightened the blue of his gaze. She felt an answering smile on her own lips and forced her mouth to firmness.

"Oh, no. Constance was greatly looking forward to this, my lord. I know she holds you in high esteem."

"I am honored." He leaned closer. "And you, Miss Collins? Do I hold a similar place in your esteem?"

"Why, why certainly." She was stammering! She cleared her throat, leaning back from him. "That is, I see every reason to admire you, my lord."

"Then I hope you will not doom me to drive alone, if your stepsister does indeed change her mind."

"She will not change her mind," Katherine promised, rising. He rose as well. "If you will excuse me, I shall see what I can do to bring her to you."

She found Eric, Bixby, and Sir Richard in Constance's room. Her stepsister was huddled in bed, the window curtains were drawn, and everyone conversed in whispers.

"What is this?" Katherine demanded from the doorway. The men quickly hushed her. Emma came up behind her with a loaded tray, and Katherine moved aside to let their housekeeper pass.

"Here, Miss Constance," the older woman said helpfully. "Cucumber compresses and some nice chamomile tea."

Bixby sidled up to Katherine. "Headache," he explained. "Not much to be done, I'm afraid."

Katherine found the timing impossible to believe. "Constance is not prone to female aches," she reminded the butler, though she kept her voice low. "What makes you think this is not a fabrication?"

From the bed, Constance moaned. To Katherine, it sounded just as theatrical as her agony on the stair a few days ago. Sir Richard and the rest obviously thought otherwise, for they exchanged sympathetic looks.

Katherine marched up to the bed and glared down at her. "Constance Templeman, do you mean to tell me you will forego a drive with Lord Borin for a miserly headache?"

Constance peered up at her, eyes brimming with tears. "Oh, Katherine," she said in an anguished whisper, "I want to go, believe me. I am utterly distraught to miss a chance to drive with his lordship." A hand fluttered to her brow, dislodging the compress Emma was trying to place.

Katherine threw up her hands and stalked back to the withdrawing room.

She schooled her face to regret before entering. "I fear Constance has been taken ill," she told Lord Borin, who had risen at the sight of her. "No doubt it will pass as quickly as Sir Richard's ailment. But I fear she will not be able to accompany you today."

"I quite understand. Shall I wait while you fetch your shawl?"

Katherine blinked. "Me? Oh, no, my lord, I cannot join you. I should see to my stepsister's needs."

"You were able to visit while Sir Richard was down," he pointed out logically.

"Yes, well, but sometimes another woman . . ." Katherine started, but his frown told her he didn't believe her. "Do you truly wish for my company?"

His smile was so warm her heart danced in her chest. "You would honor me, Miss Collins."

Telling herself she might as well do something to further their advantage, she went to fetch her bonnet and shawl.

She wasn't sure what to expect, but she thoroughly enjoyed herself. She felt like a queen riding up so high in his carriage. The breeze teased her cheeks, and the sun was warm. It was rather flattering to watch heads turn as they passed.

And her companion was as charming as she'd known he'd be. She asked after his studies years ago, his exploits since, hoping to learn more. He did not brag, but neither was he nauseatingly humble about his abilities. In fact, she got the impression that he took his good fortune in stride. She could not help envying him that and told him so. He sobered immediately.

"I had not realized until recently the drawbacks to such an existence," he replied as he drove the horses through the tree-lined paths of Hyde Park. "Tell me, Miss Collins, do you believe a gentleman is only worthwhile if he is willing to strive for a goal?"

She frowned in thought. "I would say that many gentlemen of my admittedly small acquaintance have no goal. They seem content to drift from one activity to another, always in search of something to interest them, to entertain them."

He nodded. "That is exactly what I mean. Such an existence can be pleasurable, for a time, but I find it growing stale."

Was he about to confess he would join the military? She felt her panic rising. "But surely with your fortune you could do a great deal of good," she tried. "Charities, benefits, endowed trusts."

He wrinkled his nose as if in disgust. "And let someone else manage it or have to stomach the tedious administration. Either way, my interests are hardly served."

Was it excitement he craved, then? She felt compelled to press him. "You would not do something drastic, my lord? Renounce your title? Take holy orders? Join the cavalry?"

She relaxed as he barked out a laugh. "Good God,

no! I may be an idealist, Miss Collins, but I am no martyr." He sobered again. "Though perhaps it would be better if I were. I admit to having a deuce of a time keeping to my task."

"What task is that?" she asked, curious.

"I confessed its nature to your uncle, but he seemed to want to handle the issue himself. Perhaps you should discuss the matter with him."

You can be sure I shall, she thought. Aloud she said, "Very well, my lord. But if you will not divulge the task, will you at least share with me what keeps you from it? Perhaps I can help."

"Ah, but I cannot find it in me to wish rescue," he replied with a grin. "The distraction is the company of a charming young lady."

She grinned back. "Yes, Constance is a marvel, isn't she?"

He started laughing again. "You are the most humble female it has been my good fortune to meet. Will you not allow yourself to be praised?"

He meant her? She felt herself warming and stamped down the feelings with impatience. He could not want her. It would spoil everything. "Certainly I accept praise, when it is warranted. But do not attempt to tell me I am more beautiful or charming than my stepsister, my lord. I took you for an honest man."

He shook his head, urging the horses through a knot of carriages. "I assure you, I am honest to a fault. However, if you wish to hear your stepsister praised, I will admit she is without peer."

Now why didn't that please her? For once she had managed to get him to focus on Constance. "Yes, she is," she said firmly. "She is accomplished, sweet natured, and good-hearted. She would make some fellow a marvelous wife."

There, she could not have put it more plainly unless

she proposed to the fellow on her stepsister's behalf. She glanced at him from the corner of her eye and saw him nod his golden head sagely. She should be in alt, but all she felt was a distinct lowering of her spirits.

"So," he said merrily, "we have discussed my activities and your stepsister's worth. What of you, Miss Collins?"

"Me?" She tensed. Could he suspect? She prayed her voice did not betray the rapid beat of her heart. "What do you mean?"

"Surely such a lovely young lady must have a few pastimes. What do you do for entertainment?"

If you only knew. "I fear I am far too busy managing the household for idle pastimes, my lord," she replied primly.

"Did not your stepsister say you play the harp?" he pressed.

She grimaced. "In truth, I once took great pleasure from it. Unfortunately, my mother was forced to sell my instrument when my father died. My stepfather bought me another, but it was in his town house. The new Lord Templeman has not found it convenient to have it returned."

He frowned. "But I thought your stepfather died two years ago."

"Three," she replied, and could not completely erase her bitterness. "But Lord Templeman is a very busy man. No doubt my instrument does not remain on his mind long." She shook off the depression that threatened. "It matters little. I have my hands full with the household and tutoring Eric."

"Your younger brother?" When she nodded, he continued. "He is not away at school?"

She heard the increased interest behind the tone. He must suspect Eric was the boy he had followed back to their home. "He will enter Eton fall term, we hope," she told him carefully. With any luck, he would think that her hesitancy was caused by her brother's abilities and not their financial state, which was actually the case. "Now he spends a great deal of time preparing."

She managed to maneuver the conversation back to his own childhood. As he talked, she watched the sunlight through the trees caress his face with light. The glow rivaled that which shone from his eyes as he spoke of his family. They were gone now, like her father, mother, and stepfather. He seemed just as saddened by the loss as she was. Yet growing up in Hampshire sounded more pleasant than she had thought country life to be, although she sensed a touch of loneliness behind his words. What would she have done if not for Eric and her mother at first, and then Constance and Sir Richard? Might she too have frittered away her life?

They returned to the house deep in conversation. It was with true regret that she elicited his promise to call again on Constance and waved him goodbye.

Inside, she immediately checked on her stepsister, to find the girl convincingly abed. The only sign that she had done more than sleep was her Bible lying open beside her and her writing desk on the table beside the bed. Katherine could not help noticing the list of names on the lap desk, particularly as Lord Borin's was on the top. But she could not bring herself to wake her stepsister and ask. She would have to wait until morning.

Neither could she ask her uncle about his conversation with the viscount. Eric was studying geography with Sir Richard. Bixby, helping Emma prepare the evening meal, was more interruptible. She pulled the butler aside.

"Any news on Miss Montgomery?"

He kept his voice low over the bubble of the kettle

on the stove. "The Duke of Rehmouth is interested, but has been unwilling to oust Lord Borin. It wouldn't take much to get Miss Montgomery to switch allegiance."

Katherine nodded. "See that she gets the ruby, then, as a parting gift from Lord Borin. And see that the duke is aware that she may need further consolation."

"Are you sure?" Bix pressed. "What if she won't accept the ruby?"

"If she is all that you say, she will accept it," Katherine replied in dismissal. "And any woman who would release Lord Borin for a jewel doesn't deserve him."

Eight

Alex wasn't sure whether to be pleased or annoyed. It very much looked as if everyone in the Collins household was innocent. The Bow Street Runner confirmed as much.

"Sounds like a right neighborly group," he told Alex that evening when he made his report. "Though rumor has it the youngest miss is a bit of a snob."

Alex already knew the lie of that rumor. He set his hopes on Lord Templeman, only to be disappointed again.

"None too pleasant a gentleman, to be sure," the runner said. "But I could find nothing too havey cavey about his business. Sorry, me lord, but it looks like you might be chasing the wrong goose."

So, Templeman had no reason to watch him either. Neither had Alex been able to spot anyone following him the last few days. Apparently whatever interest he had held, he now lacked. It was rather lowering. He had no mystery, and nothing to commend himself to Lord Hastings.

The one thing he had gotten from his investment of time was an appreciation for the quick mind and strong spirit of Miss Katherine Collins. He would have liked to further that acquaintance, but in doing so, he would raise expectations that he intended to offer for her. And he wasn't ready to retire to matrimony just yet.

As if to prove it to himself, he strolled over to Lydia's flat that evening. He was fully aware that he had been neglecting his mistress for several days, and fairly certain she would be thoroughly miffed about it. Most likely she would attempt to wrangle a bauble or two out of him as penance. With that thought in mind, he had stopped by the jewelers earlier in the day and picked up a ruby pendant.

As he approached the building that housed her flat, he was consoling himself with the thought that the stone would at least grant him an evening's reprieve. Time enough later to call off their arrangement. He did not think she would be distraught. Too many others were sniffing at her heels. And small wonder. Her curves were legendary. The color of her long, flowing, golden hair was not the cunning of a bottle. Those violet eyes could be cool or passionate. But for all that, he found he was not going to miss her.

He was perhaps three doors away when he sighted a tall, shabbily dressed man hurrying out of the entrance. Even in the twilight, he felt sure it was the man who had followed him.

Alex leaped forward. "Stop!"

The fellow jerked around, eyes widening, then turned to flee. Alex halted in shock. It was the Collinses' butler. He started forward again, but not before the fellow sprinted around the corner. He knew better than to try to catch him. Besides, it wasn't as if he didn't know exactly where to find him.

He glanced up at the apartment building. What connection could the Collins family have with the tenants? Was his mistress somehow involved with the plots against him? By heaven, he was becoming positively paranoid! Mind whirling, he entered the building and climbed the stairs to Lydia's flat.

Maudie, her little dark-haired maid, was surprisingly hesitant to let him in the door. Once he entered his lady's sitting room, he understood why. The Duke of Rehmouth lounged on the rose velvet settee. Only the fact that his dark hair was still pomaded in place and his black evening clothes unrumpled saved him from feeling the force of Alex's fist.

"Bit behind times, old fellow," Rehmouth said as if he noted the fire in Alex's eyes. "I came as soon as I heard the news."

"Oh?" Alex replied, forcing himself to move to the hearth and lean negligently against the pink marble fireplace. Lydia had insisted on redoing the place in shades of red, claiming it romantic. He had thought it rather endearing at the time; now he found it stifling. "What news was that?"

Before the duke could answer, Lydia sailed from the dressing room. The diaphanous morning robe that fluttered about her curvaceous form only enhanced her considerable charms. "My Lord Borin," she announced pleasantly, "you did not need to come yourself. As you can see, I am well cared for."

Rehmouth leaned farther back and smiled proprietarily. Alex fought the impulse to knock the silly smile from his face. Had he ever looked so besotted?

"I do thank you, of course," Lydia was continuing, "for the ruby. It is a lovely parting gift."

Alex stared at her. "You knew I had bought you a ruby?"

Lydia's fair brows drew together over her violet eyes. "Do you deny it? I refuse return it, so if that's why you came, you can take yourself off. You've been nothing but inattentive these past few weeks. I deserve something for my trouble."

He hoped Rehmouth was taking note of how unbecoming her rose-tinted lips looked in that petulant pout. He'd seen it far too often. Unfortunately, if he'd only seen it sooner, he wouldn't now be in this awkward position.

"I would never be so foolish as to attempt to part you from your beloved baubles," he replied. "However, I happen to be carrying the ruby I intended to give you, and I find myself curious as to why you think it already in your possession."

"Another ruby?" She licked her lips. "Certainly I would be delighted to show you the first stone. Perhaps a trade—information for the ruby you carry?"

"If it is the right information," Alex allowed. "Your Grace, would you excuse us for a moment? I promise this will be my last visit with Miss Montgomery."

The duke inclined his dark head. "Very well, but be quick about it. I have tickets to the opera."

Alex returned the nod, then took Lydia's elbow and directed her to her dressing room.

"Ah, my dear Borin, how I shall miss you," she murmured. Alex noted the moisture in her eyes. She was a talented actress, he'd give her that. She moved around the clothes that had been strewn about, costumes for her work in the theater, and out of it. The swing of her hips told him she knew he was watching. He shook his head.

"You will miss my pocketbook," he told her. "Rehmouth, unfortunately, is not quite as well heeled."

Approaching her dressing table, she turned to make a face at him. "He will be far more devoted than you were," she informed him, turning back to open one of her jewelry cases.

"Then you should shed no tear for my absence."

She snatched up a ring and held it out to him. "This was delivered a few moments ago."

So the duke had arrived before the stone. He made a mental note to ask Rehmouth who had passed on the news earlier. Now he joined her to examine the bauble. It was a large stone in an elaborate gold setting from an earlier time. Tiny diamonds ringed the center ruby. It was lovely, but not, he thought, as expensive as the pendant in his pocket.

"Did you recognize the man who delivered it?"

She shook her head. "I only caught a glimpse of him at the door. Maudie dealt with him. I assumed he was in your employ."

"Was he dressed in my livery?"

She frowned. "No, now that I think of it. But of course you might have had him dress in a common manner to avoid the gossipmongers."

"And you never doubted I would be so cold as to cut you off without coming myself?"

She had the good sense to blush. "Well, you had been distant. And I heard rumors."

Alex eyed her. "Rumors?"

"About Miss Templeman. I saw her at the theater once. A beautiful girl and an heiress as well, I hear. You are to be congratulated."

"Your congratulations are premature," he informed her. "Might I speak with Maudie?"

"Why?" she asked with a frown. "Do you doubt me?"

"Not at all," he replied truthfully. "But I didn't send this ring. And I would like to see what she knows about the fellow who did."

With obvious curiosity, she called her maid. The little woman cowered in front of Alex, as if expecting a beating. With Lydia's volatile temper, he supposed the idea wasn't too far-fetched. He spoke as gently as he could, but her trembling answers told him she knew nothing more than Lydia about the mysterious messenger.

It was little different with Rehmouth. His valet had heard from another servant that Lord Borin intended to call off the affair. Rehmouth had been only too happy to postpone his other activities and hasten to the side of the fair Lydia to persuade her of his devotion. Alex would have liked to discredit their stories, but neither seemed to have reason to lie. He left the pendant with a delighted Lydia and took his leave.

Outside, he turned up the collar of his coat against the chill wind that had blown up. Just when he thought the mystery ended, more intrigue appeared. He'd been thinking of ending his liaison with Lydia in any event, so he supposed he owed someone a favor for extracting him so neatly. But it galled him that someone would have the temerity to manage his life for him.

And why? What did it profit anyone whom he partnered? He dallied with the idea that Lydia was the person passing secrets to the foreign agents, but he could not see how. Her beauty gave her access to high circles, but it had been well known she was under his protection. Even Rehmouth had been unwilling to do more than drool until hearing Alex had thrown her off. Besides, Lydia's temper made her an unlikely agent. One needed a cool head to play at political intrigue.

As cool a head as whoever was playing with his life.

His only clue lay in his recognition of the Collinses' butler. The fellow could have had a reason to visit Lydia's apartment house—any number of other families lived above and below her. However, they did not appear to be poor enough to be a relative to the average servant, or rich enough to be acquainted with people in the same class as the Colliness. And then there was the fact that the butler bore a strong resemblance to the man who had been following him earlier.

Like it or not, his only clue led back to the Collins house. He hated to think of Richard Collins as a traitor. He'd far rather prove his innocence than his guilt. But to do either, he'd have to find a way into the house that went beyond these polite public visits. He needed to be able to search for evidence that linked the Collinses to him and told him why they might want to follow him.

His pulse quickened as he sorted through possibilities on the walk home. He did not like the idea of playing thief. Breaking windows and crawling about a darkened house sounded like an excellent way to get himself shot, and he rather pictured Miss Collins at the other end of the barrel. Sneaking inside in broad daylight while they were busy with other tasks sounded chancy at best. Forcing his way in at gunpoint would likely end with him in Bethlehem Mental Hospital.

Of course, there was seduction. His smile widened. Easy to imagine ways to get Miss Collins alone. Even easier to imagine ways to lull her into a false sense of security. He would take her in his arms and pull down that ridiculous knot of hair, letting the auburn tresses slide past his fingers. Perhaps he'd even bring a strand or two to his lips. He'd wager they were soft as silk. He'd lift the hair and kiss the back of her neck, the tender spot behind her ear, her cheek, and those tempting lips. Good God, he was getting aroused just thinking of it.

This would never do. Besides, what was he supposed to do with the rest of the family if he succeeded in gaining mastery over Miss Collins? And how was he to master her when she so easily mastered him, even in his thoughts?

The answer, luckily, awaited him at home. Retreating to his study, he had sunk into a comfortable chair and proceeded to absently thumb through correspondence that had arrived that day. The invitation from the Collinses was easy to spot.

So, Miss Templeman was having a party. He tapped the refolded paper against his lips. He had never hosted a party himself, but had seen friends and acquaintances go through the process any number of times. These events required visits from tradesmen and deliveries of wine, extra plate and cutlery, and flowers. Parties frequently required musicians and caterers, not to mention extra servants.

He could attend the party. It alone might give him sufficient opportunity to search the house. On the other hand, if the Collinses had invited him for the purpose of keeping an eye on him, he would be under surveillance. Best to go in ahead of time, while they were busy preparing.

At last, a chance to put his skills to work. He could hardly wait.

Katherine was fully prepared to wait outside her uncle's door the next day if need be to quiz him about Alex's intentions. However, Constance's revelation at the breakfast table changed all her plans.

"I thought we should host a dinner party Friday," she announced as she calmly buttered her toast.

Katherine glanced to where Bixby stood by the sideboard. He shrugged as if to say the idea was news to him as well.

"Certainly we can host a dinner," Katherine replied. "But Friday might be a bit too soon. What brought this on?"

Constance kept her gaze on the toast as she followed the butter with a thick smear of apricot preserve. "Since I had to forego the drive with Lord Borin, I thought I should try to make amends. I proposed dinner, then dancing afterward. And maybe card tables for those, like Sir Richard, not inclined to dance."

Katherine knew her smile was strained. Constance could have no idea of the amount of work necessary to pull off such an event. Between Katherine's attempts to interest Lord Borin and keep her uncle from making a fool of himself, she already had her hands full. "How clever of you, dearest," she told Constance. "A small dinner might just be the thing. Perhaps in a few weeks."

Her stepsister met her gaze at last, with a frown. "Does that mean I shall have to rescind the invitations?"

Katherine stared at her. "Invitations? When did you send invitations?" She looked at Bixby again. He shook his head, clearly as confused as she was. Constance merely smiled.

"Why yesterday, while you were driving. Eric helped me. It was quite easy. I made a list."

The list! It could only be the one she had seen last night. But there had been at least thirty names on it. If invitations had been sent, she was well and truly trapped.

Bixby did not see it that way when he caught up with her later that morning. "Might as well spend Miss Constance's money on a worthy cause," he told Katherine. "With any luck, she'll snag Borin or another fellow, and we won't have to worry about giving the fortune to Lord Templeman."

Sir Richard agreed with him when she finally managed a moment to corner her uncle. "A party might just bring the girl out of her shell," he mused.

That she could not argue. Resigned, she took the opportunity to ask her uncle about Lord Borin's discussion with him. Sir Richard shrugged.

"He seemed to think he was being followed and we had something to do with it."

Katherine swallowed. "Really? And what did you tell him?"

Her uncle was watching her, and she held herself still, hoping he would not notice how her pulse had sped. "I told him I would look into the matter. It is nonsense, is it not, Katherine?"

"Absolute nonsense," she assured him. "Now, if you will excuse me, I really must begin planning for this party."

She hurried away before he could question her further.

It took Alex a great deal of work over the next few days to put his plan into action. Giles Sloan helped him interview caterers until he found the one the Collinses were going to use. Alex then had to arrange an anonymous bribe to the fellow to allow a particular person to serve as footman for the affair. Alex thought perhaps he should have more of a disguise than simply playing a servant, but Sloan shook his head.

"People pay no notice to servants," he explained. "You shall be in livery, with a powdered wig on your head. You will look no different from any other fellow working a temporary job."

Alex couldn't quite believe that. He decided that a bit of blacking to darken his brows and some cotton padding in his cheeks to change their shape would help ensure he was not detected.

His determination to undertake the charade was only encouraged by the fact that his shadow had returned, and appeared to have been augmented. Instead of the old man or boy, now it was a far more menacing fellow—tall, muscular, and darkly dressed. Alex spotted him loitering in the street outside his town house, near White's on St. James, and on the corner near Gentleman Jackson's boxing emporium. Twice he gave chase, only to lose him far too quickly.

He had no idea whether the occurrences were connected to the Collinses. He had received no word from Sir Richard, which might mean the man had learned nothing about why Alex was being followed. On the other hand, it might mean that he'd never intended to tell Alex what he knew. It looked as if he was justified in invading their home in search of answers.

Still, the idea of his charade seemed so dashed unsporting. As a gentleman, Alex felt he owed it to Sir Richard to ask him for an explanation. Besides, he had told Miss Collins he might call again. Accordingly, the day before the party, he returned to the Collins home.

As usual, the butler met him at the door, looking as imperious as he had on the previous occasions. Alex thought he saw a look of interest flit through the fellow's eyes. He had no sooner requested a moment of Sir Richard's time, however, when there was a crash overhead.

"I shall kill him!"

Alex jumped, pulse racing. Something *was* going on in that house! As if the butler realized they had been caught, he blanched and made to close the door. "Terribly sorry, my lord. Sir Richard is out. Good day, Lord Borin."

Alex shoved his shoulder in the crack, wedging open the door. "What is it? Is everything all right?"

"Places!" This time the cry came from Katherine's voice. Footsteps clattered on the stair.

"Please, Lord Borin," the butler begged, pushing ineffectually against his shoulder. "Another time."

Alex refused to be stopped. This could be exactly what he had been looking for.

"Bixby!" Alex recognized Sir Richard's tenor, severely strained. "Fetch me my sword cane. Wellington's honor must be defended!"

Nothing would keep him out of that house. Alex gave a mighty heave, knocking the butler backward and throwing the door against the wall with a crack. He leaped over Bixby's body into the entryway.

Nine

Sir Richard halted halfway down the stairs. Katherine, poised to ascend, whirled to face Alex, blood congealing in her chest. Their secret was out. The *ton* would know that her bon vivant uncle had fallen into ruin. Below her, Bixby looked just as panicked. He scrambled to his feet and backed away from Lord Borin. She met Alex's wide-eyed gaze and noted it was nearly as crazed as her uncle's. Her heart plummeted to her feet. No doubt that was why she couldn't move as Sir Richard swept past her.

"Borin, my lad," he declared, clapping Alex on the shoulder of his well-cut camel coat. "A sight for sore eyes, to be sure. Did you read that editorial in *The Chronicle?*"

He blinked, then focused as if with difficulty on Sir Richard. She waited for him to denounce her uncle, but he merely nodded, relaxing his stance. "Claptrap," he said. "No intelligent man would give it credence. If Wellington's honor must be defended, count me in."

"Capitol," Sir Richard replied enthusiastically. "Come in, come in. Are you hungry? Thirsty? Katherine, we must have something for our guest."

"Right away, Uncle," she managed. At a nod from her, Bixby ceased dusting off his dark coat and breeches and hurried down the corridor. "This way, gentlemen," she said, waving them up toward the withdrawing room.

Sir Richard turned to comply and nearly lost his balance. Katherine started forward, but Alex slipped deftly against him as if to murmur a private word. Deep in conversation, they meandered up the stairs. Alex's wink to Katherine behind her uncle's back was her only indication that he knew the trouble he had averted.

Eric came hurrying from the library. "What happened? I was all set to beg Uncle's help as we planned. Was that Lord Borin?"

"It was indeed," Katherine replied, staring up the now-empty stair. "And I am not certain what is happening. For now, stay out of sight until I call for you."

Nodding, he scampered back to the library. Shaking her head, Katherine went to fetch Constance.

Her stepsister, however, refused to join the men. "I am to drive in a few minutes with Allison Munroe. Had you forgotten?"

"Miss Munroe will understand completely that you must wait upon Lord Borin," Katherine insisted. "She is in the middle of her first Season as well."

"I do not wish to make her understand," her stepsister replied kindly. "It is wrong to break a promise. I am disappointed that I cannot see Lord Borin today, but I will console myself with the fact that I shall see him at the party tomorrow."

Katherine wanted to press the issue, but she recognized the set to Constance's lovely mouth. Pushing her now might win the battle, but it could lose the war. Shaking her head, she hurried back to the withdrawing room. She reached the door just as Bixby arrived with refreshments.

"Let me take that," she said, smoothing down her gray poplin skirts before reaching for the tray of lemonade and cakes. "After last week, we do not wish Lord Borin to get a good look at you."

Bixby made a face. "Poor timing to have him catch me like that at Miss Montgomery's. Lucky he didn't try to follow me home."

"If he recognized you, there would have been no need to follow you home," Katherine replied. "Best let me take the refreshments in, just in case. Perhaps I can learn what he wants with Sir Richard, and what he intends to tell others."

Bixby nodded, and she entered the withdrawing room.

Both men rose from their seats on the blue velvet chairs. Her uncle looked less delighted than when he'd first sighted Lord Borin; his face was nearly as dark as the aubergine coat he wore. He did not, however, appear to have returned to his previous ire, for which she was grateful. If anything, he looked thoughtful, auburn brows gathered over his dark eyes.

The viscount, on the other hand, looked determined. His chin was set, his deep blue eyes cool. The way his arms crossed over his broad chest only strengthened her desire to know why he had come.

"Here we are, gentlemen," she declared, setting down the tray on the gilt end table and seating herself beside it with every intention of playing hostess. "Lemonade, Lord Borin?"

He sat and accepted the glass she poured with a word of thanks. Her fingers brushed his, the brief touch surprisingly warming. She made herself focus on serving her uncle as well. Still, neither man moved to continue the conversation.

"Have I interrupted?" she asked blithely. "Pray continue. Do not mind me. I just want to see to these cakes."

They eyed each other, and the cakes she passed to

them, but neither took her up on her offer to continue the conversation. She would have to try herself.

"I hope my uncle's defense of the good general did not overly concern you, Lord Borin. *The Chronicle* is often successful in its duty to arise public ire, is it not?"

He nodded, sitting back in his chair as if nothing were troubling him. "Most assuredly. I would be surprised if your uncle did not react strongly to such opposition to our valiant troops."

Sir Richard nodded as well. Katherine smiled. So much for that concern. On to the next. "And what brings you to see us today, my lord?"

The viscount took such a long sip of his lemonade before answering that she thought she might scream. "I had some news of a mutual acquaintance to share with your uncle," he said at last.

"And I appreciate it," Sir Richard replied. "I simply am not certain how to respond."

She glanced between the two of them, thoroughly mystified. "May I be of assistance?"

"No!"

She recoiled from the vehement chorus. Neither looked ready to apologize, or explain. Rising, she shook out her skirts. "I shall leave you to it, then. Good day, Lord Borin."

He rose and bowed, but she swept out without an acknowledgment.

In the corridor, she slipped against the plastered wall. Eavesdropping was unconscionably rude, but she had to know what her uncle and Lord Borin were about. If the viscount had discovered her plans for him, all was lost.

"So you have no idea why your man might want to spy on me?" he was saying.

Katherine sighed. He *had* recognized Bix. Another perfectly good operative sunk. Fortunately, she seemed to have outgrown the need or she'd have to go herself next time.

"I am sorry, Borin," her uncle replied, "but I am at a loss. I have watched the house for any skullduggery, but everyone seems immersed in planning for this party. Is it possible you are mistaken?"

Katherine held her breath and heard the viscount puff out his. "In truth," he said, "I do not know. I suppose it is possible I counted the wrong house when I first followed the boy. What do you know of your neighbors?"

Katherine let out her breath. Her neighbors were harmless, but with any luck, investigating them would keep him too busy to bother with her. She listened a few more minutes while they dissected the lives of those living on the terrace, then tripped happily away, secure in the knowledge that her scheme had not yet been discovered. She would turn her energies to making sure the party brought Constance and Lord Borin together.

Lord Templeman was not feeling nearly so secure. Borin was becoming decidedly tiresome. It had cost Templeman a pretty penny to bribe that Bow Street Runner to return a bland report of him. Just the fact that Borin would dare to have him investigated was cause enough for alarm. Such an inquiry might lead to his connection to certain dealings with foreign enterprises. Those contacts could prove lucrative, once he had used his cousin's fortune to open a few doors to more telling information.

But there Borin interfered yet again. The viscount had gone calling on the Collinses, and this after severing ties to his mistress, in the most preemptive fashion, if rumors were true. Lord Templeman's affairs and his fortune were in jeopardy. It was time to act, and he knew just the lie that would set things in motion. With any luck, within a week or two Borin would be too busy defending himself to worry about him or his cousin Constance.

Sir Richard also knew it was time to act. He waited only until the door closed behind his guest before limping to the library. He found Eric sprawled on the rug before the fire, eating some of the same cake Katherine had offered them and reading from his Latin text.

"Lord Borin nearly caught you that time, didn't he?" he asked.

The boy grinned, freckles dancing across his short nose in the firelight. "He sure did. I almost . . ." His eyes widened. "Oops."

"Oops indeed, my lad," his uncle declared, easing himself into a leather armchair beside him. "Care to tell me what's happening?"

Eric clamped his lips tight and shook his head.

Sir Richard tapped his knee. "I see. Valor in the face of the enemy. Refusing to give up state secrets. Most impressive. What if I were to try bribery?"

Eric grinned. "Take me to Astley's Royal Amphitheatre to see the horses?"

"Oh, a tall order. But I might be persuaded."

His grin faded. "Sorry, Uncle. Much as I want to see the horses, I gave my word. A gentleman never goes back on his word."

"Too true," Sir Richard commiserated. "What if I were to guess? Confirming a guess isn't going back on your word, is it?"

Eric screwed up his face in thought. "I do not think Katherine would agree."

"Perhaps not," Sir Richard allowed. "Very well, I

give up. Your honor is saved. Run along now and send your sister to me, will you?"

"All right," Eric agreed, "but be warned, Uncle. She's a lot tougher than I am."

Sir Richard had no doubt that would be the case. Just seeing how squared her shoulders were as she entered the room told him he dealt with a seasoned operative. He decided to go straight to the heart of the matter.

"You set Bixby and Eric to spy on Lord Borin. Why?"

Her pupils dilated, but she merely raised her head. "You drink yourself into a stupor most nights and put us through hell when you are awake. Do I ask your motive?"

He flinched. "Point taken, my girl. Your brother is right. You are a great deal tougher than he is."

She eyed him. "Just what did Eric tell you?"

"Not nearly enough. You should be proud of him."

"I am. For any number of reasons. Now, may I go?"

Sir Richard raised a brow. "Do you think I give up so easily? I intend to get to the bottom of this, my girl." He cocked his head to regard her. She stared stonily back. "Has Lord Borin dallied with you, Katherine?" he pressed. "Are you after revenge?"

"Good heavens, no!" Her denial was vehement, but he sensed the truth with relief. "Lord Borin is a gentleman, Uncle. He would never knowingly compromise a lady, and if he did so inadvertently, I have no doubt he would take responsibility."

"Then why harass the poor fellow?"

She sighed. "We have stopped. Neither Bix nor Eric shall follow him again. Is that sufficient for you?"

"Not in the slightest. I wish to know what drove you to such drastic measures."

She threw up her hands. "Is it not evident? Constance refuses to marry. She has less than five weeks before she loses her fortune. I have paraded every eligible gentleman in London before her, and she does not so much as notice. I begin to think she wishes for poverty!"

"More likely she is unaware of the consequences," Sir Richard replied thoughtfully. "I shall speak to her. In truth, I had forgotten the time was drawing near. Will she truly be twenty this June?"

Katherine nodded. "And no closer to the altar than at her debut, I fear."

"Then you would be twenty-two," he mused. "And no closer to the altar yourself."

She reddened, and he knew he had scored a hit. The knowledge brought him no joy.

"My willingness to wed is not the issue," she told him tartly. "Do you wish to see my stepfather's money go to his hideous nephew?"

"Frankly, I do not care. But you obviously do. Perhaps I should look more closely at our finances again. Are we approaching beggary?"

She dropped her gaze. "We will not starve. But we will have to move to another part of London, or the country, and we will have to release Emma and Bixby."

"As bad as that?" Sir Richard frowned. Why hadn't he realized it? It was one thing to overlook his niece's age—children grew up all too quickly. It was another to overlook their financial well-being. He tried to remember the last time he had paid a bill, and couldn't recall. But if they were in arrears, surely he'd have been dunned. He didn't remember any threatening notes or demanding visitors. He suddenly realized that he didn't even remember what day it was. The realization stunned him.

Katherine's gaze on his face recalled him to the conversation. He cleared his throat. "I begin to see why you are concerned, Katherine. But you cannot force Constance into marriage to save us."

"Nor would I!" she immediately protested. "I have tried to find a man so wonderful she cannot refuse him."

"Lord Borin," he guessed.

She nodded. "He is affable, generous, and kind. He has an excellent fortune in his own right, so she cannot say he is after hers. And you cannot deny he is kind on the eyes."

"Certainly not." He also could not deny that Katherine seemed more than a little attracted herself. "But you bring me back to my original question. Why spy on the fellow?"

"I had to be certain he was the right choice for Constance," she all but pleaded. "I also had to determine whether there were any obstacles to their courtship or whether we had anything of worth to tempt him to marriage."

He frowned. "What you describe begins to sound like entrapment. What exactly did you plan for the poor fellow?"

"Nothing heinous, I promise you! I thought if Constance were to wear a scent he preferred or dress in shades of his favorite color, he might be attracted enough to come closer. Am I not entitled to gather data before undertaking such an activity as helping Constance go courting?"

"I find it difficult to believe all young ladies have such information on their perspective bridegrooms, unless of course, they simply ask."

She ignored the pointed suggestion. "Few young ladies have to contend with the factors we face," she countered. "Can you say you are sorry we managed to get him to call?"

"I find him quite companionable," Sir Richard assured her. "But I am not going to marry him. And you cannot blame the fellow for wondering what goes on.

Particularly with rumors of foreign spies among the *Haut Ton*."

Her eyes widened. "Foreign spies? What is this?"

"A rumor only, as far as I know, but a persistent one. Apparently several members of Parliament have been approached, those who have ties to the War Office. Lord Hastings is surely investigating. But you can see why being followed might make Lord Borin jittery."

"Certainly, but as I said, we have stopped."

"That is not all you will stop." He affixed her with a firm stare, watching her lower her gaze to the carpet. It had been a long time since he had had to play the patriarch. Indeed, he wasn't certain he had ever played the role. Still, he could not allow her to worry herself to the point at which she took such risks.

"From now on," he told her, "I will take responsibility for this family. That is my right and duty as a gentleman."

"Yes, Uncle," she murmured.

"I expect you to focus on what young ladies are supposed to focus upon—determining how they will live the rest of their lives and with whom they will live it. You can trust me to keep us afloat."

"Yes, Uncle," she said again.

His heart went out to her, but he had to get her to see the folly of her ways. "You are a bright girl, Katherine. I expect you to support me in this."

She raised her gaze at last, staring at him as firmly as he did her. "I will support you, Uncle. It will be a pleasure to have the burden relieved. But you had better prove yourself up to it. Someone has to see to the well-being of this family. If you cannot or will not, I will."

Ten

Katherine did not enjoy being scolded like a child. But she could not complain that her uncle had awoken to his duty at last. They went through the books the next morning and confirmed that her estimates were correct. He took some of the money from her mother to invest in the Exchange in the hope that they might improve their fortunes. She could tell, however, that he was not optimistic about their chances in so short a time.

She thought she might get him to help elsewhere, but he threw up his hands at the suggestion of assisting with the preparations for the party.

"I may have learned how to quarter and provision troops," he said, "but I would not presume to intrude on your territory, Colonel."

In truth, she didn't mind his retreat. After discussions with Constance, they had determined that the event should be a ball with a buffet supper to be served at midnight. Thirty people had accepted their invitations, with a few more men than women, which she hoped would mean that most of the ladies would get to dance. The preparations were nearly done. She had devised a menu, helped the caterer shop for foodstuffs, selected additional plate and silver, and ordered wine and flowers. She had seen Constance fitted for a new gown and brushed off a spruce silk gown of her mother's for herself. She had interviewed and hired musicians and selected a number of dances they were to play. By the day of the ball, all she had to do was confirm details with the caterer.

Mr. Lloyd was a fussy man, shaped like a child's ball and just as brightly colored in his lemon coat and eggplant trousers. He questioned her on any number of matters, but seemed satisfied that she knew her mind. When she finished late in the morning, she went upstairs intending to spend a few hours tutoring Eric before dressing for the ball. Instead, she found Bixby waiting for her on the first-floor landing. Putting his finger to his lips, he nodded toward the study.

Her heart sank. Was her uncle drunk again? Sir Richard had been so good. He had taken no more than a glass or two of wine in the evening. But if he overimbibed today, she would have a devil of a time hiding it from their guests. Almost afraid of what she would find, she tiptoed to the door and peered in.

It was not Sir Richard in the room. Instead, she watched in amazement as a footman with a powdered wig and fat cheeks rifled through the papers on her uncle's desk. The impudence! Before Bixby could stop her, she straightened her back and marched into the room.

"Here, now, fellow, what do you think you are doing?"

His head jerked up. Eyes like the sky at dusk met her own before being hastily dropped.

"Sorry, mum," he muttered in a rough-edged voice. "Mr. Lloyd thought he might of left the menu up 'ere."

She kept her face stern though her heart raced. "Well, he didn't. Return to your duties." She watched as he shambled humbly out. When she was certain he had gone down the stairs, she hurried out to meet her butler.

"Bix, tell me I am mad. Was that not Viscount Borin?"

The butler nodded with a grin. "God bless you, Miss Katherine, but I'm sure of it. He's too blatant to miss."

"Well, I wouldn't have noticed him if you had not pointed him out. I trusted Mr. Lloyd to choose the appropriate staff."

He nodded. "No doubt Lord Borin was counting on that. What do you think he's about?"

"Trying to figure out why you and Eric have been following him, I would guess." She paused, thinking, but could see no other reason. Besides, outside her plan, they had nothing to hide.

"What should we do, then?" Bixby pressed. "Call him out?"

She giggled. "Somehow I hate to spoil his fun. I imagine he's quite enjoying his moments of espionage. Yet I cannot have him discover our War Office."

"I quite agree," Bixby replied with a shudder. "Maybe I can simply keep him busy until he leaves."

Katherine grinned. "Why, Bix, what a delightful idea. If Lord Borin wants to play footman, we should certainly give him a taste for the role."

Alex found that he was thoroughly enjoying himself. Mr. Lloyd had been told enough about the deception to know to exempt this particular footman from much work. He did not, of course, know that the footman was a nobleman in disguise. In fact, Alex had the impression the fellow thought the footman was some nobleman's by-blow who needed gainful employment. Whatever the case, Alex merely had to stand about and look officious.

On various pretenses, he had already searched the library and the study. Sir Richard had gone out to his club, and the brother was apparently in the schoolroom. Wherever Alex looked, he found nothing incriminating, but there were still the upper floors. He simply had to avoid any more interruptions as he had just had from Miss Collins.

His heart had nearly stopped when she stormed into the room, head high. It had nearly leaped from his chest when he thought for a moment she had recognized him. But she had sent him about his tasks, and for that he had to be thankful. Miss Collins was a delicious distraction, but he had other things to attend to.

He had, however, developed a greater respect for Miss Collins's abilities. He was amazed at the number of details the party entailed, and how many of them had been completed in a relatively short time. According to Mr. Lloyd and the others, the feat was entirely the work of one Miss Katherine Collins. Now, with the guests due to arrive in a few hours, there were no confused directions, no sense of panic or even anxiety. People knew their duties and did them promptly. The food that was cooking looked delicious, the decorations delightful. He could almost regret he was going to miss the event.

He changed his opinion that afternoon. Bixby cornered him as he helped Mr. Lloyd lay out the silver.

"You there, fellow. You seem to have some muscle. Come with me."

Mr. Lloyd stepped helpfully forward. "If I may, Mr. Bixby, I need James here. Perhaps one of the others . . ."

Bixby frowned, looking down his long nose and drawing himself up to his full height. "Do you have a particular preference for this fellow, sir?"

Around him, the other footmen exchanged glances.

Alex met the gaze of his so-called employer. He could not risk discovery. Mr. Lloyd must have read the message, for he drew himself up as well. "Certainly not! I simply do not like having my people commandeered."

"You will like less the report I give Miss Collins if you are uncooperative," Bixby informed him, making the man blanch. "Now, come along, James, is it? I haven't got all day."

Alex followed him upstairs to the familiar withdrawing room. Bixby waved a hand to encompass the settee, chairs, and side tables the room boasted.

"Miss Collins has determined that this room would be more suitable for the dancing," he explained. "Move all the furniture to the walls and roll up the rug. I'll bring the polish."

"By myself?" Alex asked, glancing at the many pieces of furniture.

Bixby raised a brow. "Is there some problem, James? I assumed a strapping fellow like yourself would be used to hard work. Is there some reason I should exempt you?"

A disinclination to maim myself? That would hardly do. The other footmen did their tasks and said nothing. He had to play the role if he was to get his answers. He dropped his gaze. "No, Mr. Bixby. I'll 'op right to it."

It took him over an hour to finish the task. He tried to slip away twice to continue his quest, but once he ran into Bixby and the other time Miss Collins. The butler had merely scowled, but Alex's sprite had eyed him with a raised brow as if she began to suspect he was not the footman he appeared to be. He hurried back to the room and threw himself into his work to prove otherwise. Finally, when he could see his face in the walnut flooring, he rose to stretch cramped muscles. Turning to go, he met his sprite once again.

He thought she might praise his work, but she merely glanced around the room and sighed. "Still not enough room. It simply will not do. Put it all back."

"Back?" Alex stared at her.

She frowned, and he remembered to drop his gaze humbly. "Yes, back. I apologize, James, I did not realize you were hard of hearing." She raised her voice and moved her hands in pantomime. "PUT IT BACK!"

"I'm not . . ." Alex began, but Mr. Bixby appeared in the doorway.

"Is something wrong, miss?"

"Yes," she replied with a sigh of regret. "Apparently poor James here is hard of hearing. I was asking him to return the room to the way it was. It will not do for the dancing after all."

"Ah, very well, then." Now Bixby too began to shout. "THERE YOU ARE, JAMES! MISS COLLINS WANTS YOU TO PUT IT ALL BACK!"

"So I heard," Alex quipped as they left him to his task.

The rest of the afternoon fared no better. He no sooner finished the room than he was hustled off to sweep the front step. He felt hideously exposed as people strolled past, but no one made any remarks or even looked curious. Perhaps servants really were invisible unless they called undue attention to themselves. He felt sufficiently encouraged to try once more to break away for the upstairs, but Bixby cornered him neatly and set him to carrying tubs of water to the second floor so that Miss Templeman could arrange flowers.

Neither did he have a moment after that. He polished windows and shined silver. He rubbed oil in newel posts that already looked shiny to him. He carried Miss Templeman's arrangements to the sitting room and placed them no less than six times as Miss Collins uncharacteristically dithered about where they would show to best advantage.

His eyes burned from the perfume of the flowers and the tang of the lemon polish. His fingernails were broken and discolored. His muscles ached, and he seemed to have developed a permanent cramp in his right shoulder. Still he did not get a chance at the upper floors. He decided to make one last try after dinner when the family would be changing. It wasn't until he sat down with the other servants for some well-deserved dinner of his own, however, that he began to suspect they were on to him.

He had barely taken a grateful bite of the savory stew the housekeeper Emma served the staff when Miss Collins burst into the room, eyes convincingly wide in panic. They all rose.

"Mr. Lloyd," she cried, "the musicians are here. I completely forgot about erecting a platform. I must have assistance. Give me James."

Mr. Lloyd was obviously resigned to the popularity of his new employee. He sighed. "But of course, madam."

Alex wanted to argue. The smell of the stew set his stomach to growling. But they were all looking at him expectantly. He had no choice but to follow her out.

"THIS WAY!" she shouted, waving a hand toward the yard. He almost corrected her again, but decided it wasn't worth the argument for the few more moments he intended to be in her presence. Following her, he found himself in an old carriage house. She motioned to the wall, where rested a set of large oak planks that had probably been used to raise the carriage of the previous owners for repairs. "SEE THOSE?" she shouted. "CARRY THEM TO THE HOUSE!"

He frowned, moving closer to eye the boards. They were heavy and dusty. "I think we'd do better with a couple men."

She moved to lay a hand on his arm. "Oh, James, I am certain you can handle these yourself."

Inadvertently he met her gaze and saw the merriment in her gray eyes. She was laughing at him! She knew! Had she intended him to earn the blisters he could feel on his palms? Well, two could play at this game. If she wanted to watch him work, he'd be happy to oblige. He stepped politely back.

"Mayhap you're right, miss," he said humbly. "But 'twould be a real shame to ruin Mr. Lloyd's fine livery." He began to unbutton his coat.

"What are you doing?" Was it his imagination that she seemed a bit breathless?

"Removing my coat, miss. To lift something so heavy a fellow needs room to move."

She backed away from him as he pulled off the coat. He held it out to her, and she snatched it from him. "I'll wait in the house," she snapped, backing toward the door as if she could not take her eyes off his white shirt.

"What?" he shouted, unbuttoning his cuffs to roll them up. "Did you say something about going out, miss? Please don't leave me. I need ye to point out the way to go."

"Now what are you doing?" she all but gasped as he removed his cravat and opened the top button of his shirt. She stared at him, obviously fascinated. He flexed his muscles as if in a stretch, and her eyes widened. Hiding a grin, he bent to heft the timber onto his shoulder.

"Lead on," he told her.

She skittered out of the carriage house as if the building were on fire. He followed her into the house and up the stairs to the sitting room, where he set the plank down. There were no musicians in sight. Instead, conspicuous under the windows was a neat platform draped in white.

"Fancy that," he said. "You didn't need this after all. Maybe you'd like me to carry it back down for you?"

"Yes, perhaps that would be best," she agreed, swallowing.

He bent to pick up the beam and paused, then rose, staring at his shoulder. "Now look there. I've gone and dirtied my shirt. Perhaps I should remove that as well, before I get more dust on it."

She swallowed again. "Yes, perhaps you should."

The minx. She was still enjoying herself. He rolled his shoulders and watched her catch her lower lip with her teeth. And such a nice lower lip it was—rounded, rosy, tender. Before he knew it, he closed the distance between them and pulled her into his arms.

Her kiss was as sweet as he'd expected, her breath a soft whisper against his mouth. Her curves nestled into him as if designed to fit his body. He reveled in the feel of her until he felt her hands push against his chest. He raised his head.

"Are all footmen so bold?" she murmured, eyes wide.

"Only when their mistresses are so very desirable," he promised.

"Mistress!" she gasped and pulled hastily away. "I am not your mistress, Lord Borin, in any sense of the word." She threw his coat at him.

He caught it neatly. "No, you are not," he agreed, shrugging into it. "And that kiss was all the payment I need for the near slavery you put me through today."

"If you pretend the role of footman, my lord, you

cannot be surprised when you are asked to play the part."

"And when you send your staff to spy on me, you cannot be surprised when I retaliate in kind."

She paled. "There was nothing nefarious about my actions. If a man shows interest in my stepsister, should I not make sure he is a gentleman?"

"Your stepsister? I showed no interest in her. My interest has been in the reason you chose to spy on me. That started long before I ever set foot at your door. Do you care to explain?"

She stepped up to him and put a hand on his chest. Though the coat lay between them, he fancied he could feel the gentleness of her touch.

"My guests will be arriving shortly," she said. "I cannot explain as I should. Will you wait on us tomorrow, my lord, say three o'clock? I promise to tell all then."

Could he trust her? Those upturned gray eyes were deep with unspoken emotions. He thought he saw regret, concern, interest, and desire. Were any of them true? Or was this still a game she played? The only way to know was to take her up on her offer.

"Very well," he said. "We will speak of this again, tomorrow."

Eleven

Katherine wasn't sure how she made it through the rest of the evening. She smiled and danced and talked of commonplaces with her guests as if nothing had happened. Her body miraculously kept functioning when she was certain she had left her heart in Lord Borin's hands.

Oh, but his kiss had been wonderful—warm, filling, heady. Why should that surprise her? From the beginning she had thought him a magnificent specimen of manhood. Why would his kiss be any less magnificent?

What she hadn't expected was her reaction. She had chosen him for Constance, after all. It was a logical, dispassionate choice. He had face, fortune, and family to recommend him. She hadn't involved her own preferences in the equation. Why then did her heart beat faster when he took off his coat, her face heat when he bared his arms? Why did her mind persist in wondering whether the rest of him was so marvelously strong and supple? Why did her hands itch to smooth over that bare skin or stroke the hairs that peered from the V of his open shirt? She certainly shouldn't revel in the way their bodies melded together or their lips meshed. Above all, she should lose herself in his kiss, wishing never to part.

But she'd done all those things and more, and she very much feared she'd do them all again given the opportunity. She did not know whether he was merely flirting or whether he too felt the stirrings of something more powerful. Either way, these feelings could spell their doom. Constance must marry, and Lord Borin was not only the perfect candidate, but the only man in whom she'd shown interest. They didn't have time to wait for someone else to appear.

Constance was, of course, disappointed when Lord Borin did not attend the ball. Given Katherine's discovery of him, she realized he could hardly make an appearance. In fact, he had left after promising to call on the morrow. When next she saw him, she would have to go carefully. Simply explaining would likely wound his male consequence. Perhaps she should paint Constance as a poor waif. Some fellows seemed to like to play the knight errant. She could almost see Lord Borin in the role. For now, she had to make his excuses to her stepsister.

"He sent word he had some unexpected exertions during the day," she told Constance. "No doubt it had something to do with a horse or his boxing. He said he would call tomorrow."

To her relief, Constance did not press her. She seemed satisfied that he would be calling. Katherine attended her through the party and then made several arrangements before retiring to bed. She wanted to be ready when the viscount called.

He arrived promptly at three. Gone were all traces of the gangly, fat-cheeked footman. He was his usual handsome self, in a cinnamon coat of wool superfine and tan trousers. He bowed to her and Constance. She didn't think it her imagination that he seemed disappointed that he was not to meet with her alone. He would simply have to wait. Constance would have her time first.

"We missed you last night, my lord," her stepsister murmured with a flutter of her golden lashes.

"I regret that I could not attend," he replied graciously. "But I am certain you had any number of admirers to keep you busy."

Katherine watched as Constance simpered. "You are too kind. There *were* a number of gentlemen in attendance. Mr. Kevin Whattling asked after you, and I am certain Mr. Everett Wardman would have if he hadn't been smitten with Katherine."

Katherine felt herself blush at the reminder of how the slender Mr. Wardman had puffed his way through no less than two country dances with her.

Alex smiled. "Yes, I have noticed your stepsister has that effect on people."

She could feel her blush deepening, but did not return his compliment. He waited a moment, then apparently realizing she would not speak, he engaged Constance once more in discussion of the party. She sat quietly as they continued to converse about commonplaces. As she had planned, Eric poked his head around the doorpost a few minutes later, and she nodded. He squared his shoulders and marched into the room, bowing before the viscount, who raised a brow.

"Lord Borin," Katherine said. "May I present my brother, Eric Collins?"

Alex rose and bowed before shaking her brother's hand. Her heart could not help but warm at how seriously he took Eric. "Mr. Collins, a pleasure, sir."

"Your servant, my lord," Eric responded with equal formality. "And may I say you have a smashing set of blacks. They look to be real goers."

"What an excellent judge of horseflesh you are, Collins. They are my personal favorites in my stables."

"Tattersall's?" Eric asked.

"But of course."

He puffed out a wistful breath. Katherine had to jerk her head to encourage him to continue with the plan they had set. He grimaced as if recalling himself. "Sorry to intrude. May I borrow my stepsister? My uncle has need of her."

Constance frowned, rising. "Now? How odd. Excuse me, Lord Borin. I promise to return shortly."

Eric looked as if he would like to return as well, but Katherine shook her head once and he deflated. She breathed a sigh as they left the room.

"Another subterfuge?" the viscount asked. "Was that necessary?"

"I fear so. You see, my stepsister has no knowledge of what I did. And I prefer to keep it that way." She took a deep breath and hurried on. "I would like your word as a gentleman that you will never tell anyone what I am about to divulge."

He sobered as he reseated himself. "You have my word, madam."

She took another breath and went on to explain the situation with Lord Templeman and Constance. She tried to paint the picture of Constance in need, desperate, searching. Watching him, she saw no signs that she had succeeded in touching his heart. His jaw remained tight, his eyes dark and passionless.

"So you see," she concluded, "I was left with no choice but to find her a suitable husband."

"Certainly I see your concern," he replied, "and I applaud your interest in caring for your stepsister. Perhaps, however, you should simply ask the next gentleman his intent rather than following him about."

The next gentleman. He did not understand. Why

could he not see Constance's worth? "I am certain you are correct," she told him, "but I fear there will be no other gentleman. At least, not in time."

"I am sorry for your problem, my dear, but I will not sacrifice myself for your stepsister."

"But why is it such a sacrifice?" she pressed, perplexed. "You could not ask for a lovelier bride or a more devoted one. And her fortune is huge."

"I will not enter into a debate over Miss Templeman's merits. Suffice it to say that I am as finicky in my bride as your stepsister is in her groom. I will help you in any other way I may, but I cannot marry Miss Templeman."

All that planning, wasted! He would never submit now. She could hear the determination in his voice. His precious male consequence was more wounded than she had guessed. Men were entirely unreasonable once they reached that state, she knew from experience. Her disappointment must have shown on her face, for he reached out to pat her hand.

"There now, Miss Collins. It is done. No more secrecy between us. You can call back the fellow you've had following me the last few days."

Katherine started. "Someone else has been following you?"

He smiled. "Very convincing. You almost make me believe you had nothing to do with the man who dogged my steps the last few nights. And he was good. I very nearly missed him as well. But I am on to you, my dear."

Katherine felt cold all over as she shook her head. "My lord, I promise you, no one in my household has followed you in days. If you do not believe me, think back to your experience yesterday. You must have seen that Bixby is our only male servant."

He frowned as if realizing she spoke the truth. "Then who?"

"I do not know. Perhaps you should inform Bow Street."

He nodded. "Yes, of course. Forgive me. I naturally assumed you had had a hand in it."

Of course he would make that assumption. Most likely he had never had the misfortune to meet a managing female like her before. But the thought that someone might be after him for nefarious purposes made her blood congeal in her veins.

"This is horrid!" she cried, rising to pace. "Why should you be followed? Could my work have somehow encouraged others to think you carry valuables? Will you be set upon by cutthroats?"

He rose to catch her by the shoulders. His touch somehow managed to stave off the worst of her chill. "Do not blame yourself. I am certain there is a logical explanation, and it has nothing to do with you. Besides, I can take care of myself."

"The spies!" She pulled away from him to bring a hand to her mouth. "You are their next target!"

He chuckled, and she was surprised at the bitterness in the sound. "Oh, no, Miss Collins. These foreign agents you have no doubt heard rumors of could have no interest in me. I used to think I was made for adventure, but the last few days have proven to me that I am not cut out for espionage, as someone else once pointed out. No one wishes me ill. When I die, it will likely be from some old man's disease like gout. That is, if I do not die of boredom first."

Before she could respond, Constance bustled back into the room. "So sorry to have kept you waiting, my lord."

"I would wait an eternity for the right woman," he replied, turning to kiss her hand. She dimpled. "Sadly, however," he continued, "I find I have another engagement. I must take my leave of you."

As Constance's face fell, Katherine shook herself. He was no doubt right. There was a logical explanation for this new shadow. Perhaps after seeing Bixby or Eric behind him for so long, he had merely conjured the image of another. In any event, she should trust him to care for himself. At the moment, the most important thing was to get him to call again.

"Oh, how disappointing," her stepsister was saying. "Well, of course you must go if you have another appointment. Will we see you again soon, my lord?"

"I expect my estate to keep me busy the next few days," he replied, moving toward the door. "Perhaps after that."

Katherine's heart ached to watch her stepsister hurry after him. "But surely you will be about in society. We will see you at balls, the theater? Perhaps Almack's?"

"Possibly," he allowed, pausing as if afraid to be impolite. "I tend to run in a different pack, I fear."

"But we have some acquaintances in common," Constance protested. "Mr. Whattling, Mr. Sloan, the Willstencrafts." The girl reminded Katherine so much of a loyal hound that she nearly cried aloud.

Lord Borin seemed to be similarly moved. The coolness of his face lessened, his lips moving into a smile. "Yes, of course. Do you plan to attend Lady Janice's ball next week? Perhaps I might see both of you there."

"Assuredly," Constance promised. His gaze, however, sought Katherine's. He looked to her for understanding. She took a breath and nodded. He bowed and left.

Constance let out a sigh. "What a very presentable gentleman. We must encourage him to keep calling."

Katherine agreed, but she found it hard to hope after their conversation.

Take a Trip Back to the Romantic Regent Era of the Early 1800's with

4 FREE

Zebra Regency Romances!

(A $19.96 VALUE!)

4 FREE books are yours!

PLUS YOU'LL SAVE ALMOST $4.00 EVERY MONTH WITH CONVENIENT FREE HOME DELIVERY!

We'd Like to Invite You to Subscribe to Zebra's Regency Romance Book Club and Give You a Gift of 4 Free Books as Your Introduction! (Worth $19.96!)

If you're a Regency lover, imagine the joy of getting 4 FREE Zebra Regency Romances and then the chance to have these lovely stories delivered to your home each month at the lowest price available! Well, that's our offer to you and here's how you benefit by becoming a Regency Romance subscriber:

- **4 FREE** Introductory Regency Romances are delivered to your doorstep

- 4 BRAND NEW Regencies are then delivered each month (usually before they're available in bookstores)

- Subscribers save almost $4.00 every month

- You also receive a **FREE** monthly newsletter, which features author profiles, discounts, subscriber benefits, book previews and more

- No risks or obligations...in other words, you can cancel whenever you wish with no questions asked

Join the thousands of readers who enjoy the savings and convenience offered to Regency Romance subscribers. After your initial introductory shipment, you receive 4 brand-new Zebra Regency Romances each month to examine for 10 days. Then, if you decide to keep the books, you'll pay the preferred subscriber's price.

It's a no-lose proposition, so return the FREE BOOK CERTIFICATE today!

Say Yes to 4 Free Books!
Complete and return the order card to receive this $19.96 value, ABSOLUTELY FREE!

If the certificate is missing below, write to:
Regency Romance Book Club
P.O. Box 5214, Clifton, New Jersey 07015-5214
or call TOLL-FREE 1-800-770-1963
Visit our website at www.kensingtonbooks.com.

FREE BOOK CERTIFICATE

YES! Please rush me 4 Zebra Regency Romances without cost or obligation. I understand that each month thereafter I will be able to preview 4 brand-new Regency Romances FREE for 10 days. Then, if I should decide to keep them, I will pay the money-saving preferred subscriber's price for all 4...that's a savings of 20% off the publisher's price. I may return any shipment within 10 days and owe nothing, and I may cancel this subscription at any time. My 4 FREE books will be mine to keep in any case.

Name _____

Address _____ Apt. _____

City _____ State _____ Zip _____

Telephone ( ) _____

Signature _____
(If under 18, parent or guardian must sign.)

RN052A

Terms and prices subject to change. Orders subject to acceptance by Regency Romance Book Club.
Offer valid in U.S. only.

Treat yourself to 4 FREE Regency Romances!

A
$19.96
VALUE...
FREE!

No
obligation
to buy
anything,
ever!

PLACE
STAMP
HERE

lll..l..l.lll..l.ll.l.l.l..l.l..l.l..ll.l..lll..l

REGENCY ROMANCE BOOK CLUB
Zebra Home Subscription Service, Inc.
P.O. Box 5214
Clifton NJ 07015-5214

"We must dress with care for this ball," her stepsister continued. "Both of us."

Katherine shook her head. "What I wear can make little difference. I am not courting, if you will recall."

To her surprise, Constance did not demur. "And does not your showing reflect upon me?" she challenged, hands on hips.

Katherine frowned. "I had never thought so."

"Then think. I saw the way Lord Borin looked to you just now. It is your approval he seeks. If you wish him to continue calling, you must encourage him. We must give him every reason to wish to further the acquaintance."

With that, she could not argue.

Indeed, she did not fight her stepsister when Constance insisted on fitting one of her dresses to Katherine. It was a soft green silk that whispered as she moved. The cap sleeves and low neckline made her feel scandalously unclothed, but she had to own the feeling was not entirely unwelcome. She would have been quite pleased with the dress if she hadn't kept thinking how her stepsister would react if Lord Borin did not respond to their overtures and refused to continue to call.

The night of the ball she could not help being pleased when Sir Richard decided to join them. They made a merry threesome in the hired coach, and it was only when she was standing with Constance at the edge of the ballroom that she remembered how important this night could be. But then they were surrounded by gentlemen begging for a dance and she was more than a little surprised to find that many were interested in partnering her. She was more pleased to see Constance led off by the handsome Marquis DeGuis. Perhaps they didn't need Lord Borin's services after all.

The thought of never seeing him again spoiled the next two dances for her.

Sir Richard smiled as he watched his wards dance. Katherine was finally dressed in something more fitting to a pretty young woman than a matron. Constance was more lively than usual; to his eye, she outshone every other young lady in the room. Both were much sought after. He'd need to be on his toes to make sure no young fellow lost his head and took liberties. He grimaced as his thigh reminded him just how hard staying on his toes was going to be.

But it was not entirely the young fellows for whom he worried. He spotted his old supervisor, Lord Hastings, in the crowd, and noted the strategic placement of Allistair Fenwick, Lord Trevithan, and Davis Laughton. Trev and Davy were two of his lordship's top men, more often to be found in the field than in London society. That they were here tonight could only mean the rumors of the foreign spy were true or they wanted to prevent the rumors from coming true.

He glanced about the room again, wondering which smiling face masked a traitor. The Willstencraft family, holder of the Marlton earldom, were generally high sticklers. They were also highfliers. Gilt dripped from the candle sconces on the Chinoiserie walls, the scrolled backs of the chairs in the dowager's circle, the branches of the chandeliers overhead. The dance floor was of Italian marble, the hearth of Indonesian teak. Every attendee was draped in silk and satin and finest wool. Gentlemen raised fluted crystal in toast to bejeweled ladies who dimpled at the compliment. Strains of Brahms floated on the perfumed air. Nearly everyone seemed to be having a marvelous time.

Only two faces in the crowd looked less than pleased

to be among the select group. One belonged to Constance's cousin. Lord Templeman was glowering as the Marquis DeGuis favored the girl with a second dance. No reason to wonder at his concern. Sir Richard knew that Katherine was correct in her assumption that Templeman was already counting his fortune. He rather hoped Constance did settle on someone, if for no other reason than to cheat the odious fellow out of the money.

The other person who was obviously distressed surprised him, however, for it was Lord Borin. The handsome lord stood at the side of the ballroom and glowered almost as darkly as Lord Templeman, but it appeared to be Katherine who had earned his censure. Sir Richard glanced at his niece again and saw only a smiling young woman. As he watched, she seemed to notice Lord Borin's gaze on her. She stiffened. Then she purposely brightened her smile and fluttered her lashes at the gentleman who was partnering her. The poor fellow actually missed a step so taken was he with the sight. Borin grabbed a flute from a passing footman and quaffed the contents.

What was this? Borin jealous of attention to Katherine? Sir Richard smiled. What a lovely end to this mess that would make. He would have to see what he could do to help things along.

If he knew those two, he'd have his work cut out for him.

Twelve

Alex was not enjoying the ball in the slightest. He could see Lord Hastings, Trevithan, and Laughton casually circulating, and knew exactly what they were about. They were attempting to get to the bottom of this rumor, and they suspected the culprit was at the ball. Instead of flitting about like a blasted gadfly, he should be helping. But after Lord Hastings's refusal, he wasn't sure how welcome his assistance might be.

Even worse, however, was the way all the gentlemen were ogling Miss Collins. He knew one kiss did not tie her to him for life, particularly when he had gone out of his way to pretend the kiss had not affected him. Truth be told, he'd thought of it more than once the last few days. He had thought her beauty underappreciated, but now that the male half of the *ton* had opened their eyes, he found himself wishing they'd find other pastimes. It was one thing to discover a rare beauty; it was quite another to watch the population drool over it. He should be pleased, but he had to stop himself from rushing to her side and beating off her admirers with a stick. She must have noticed him glaring, for she found new ways to encourage the fellows and add to his torment.

He was ready to march up to the chit and demand

his turn to dance with her when he found her stepsister at his side. Miss Templeman was lovely in a gown of soft blue that matched her expressive eyes, and he thought again that her cousin would likely lose his fortune that night.

She dropped a graceful curtsy. "Good evening, my lord. I trust you are enjoying the ball."

"Enjoyment," he replied, "is the least of my emotions, Miss Templeman."

She obviously took his statement as a positive one, for she nodded. "I noticed, however, that you do not dance."

She sounded wistful. He managed a polite smile. "But you do. I do not believe you have sat out a single set."

She blushed. "Indeed, I have not. And I find myself a bit overheated. I thought perhaps a walk on the terrace would be refreshing. Might I request your company, my lord?"

His company? Walks along moonlit terraces were reserved for lovers. Was she trying to manipulate him into compromising her?

"Did your stepsister put you up to this?" he demanded.

She paled. "Katherine? Why would you think this has anything to do with her?"

"Your reaction betrays you. You may tell Miss Collins that I have had quite enough of her interference in my life. No, wait. I think it would give me greater satisfaction to tell her myself."

She caught the arm of his evening black as he started past. "Oh, please, Lord Borin. Do not confront Katherine. This was entirely my idea, I promise you. I am being terribly bold, I know, but I must speak with you alone. I thought this would be the best way to achieve that. But I haven't Katherine's flare for subterfuge, worse luck." Her lower lip trembled, and he could see tears pooling in her eyes. "Please won't you let me explain myself?" she begged.

What gentleman could resist such a plea? Even if he had not been a gentleman, he could not have ignored his curiosity. He tucked her arm in his. "Very well, Miss Templeman. But I cannot take much more of this intrigue."

"I promise to tell you all," she replied. Together, they moved to the edge of the room and slipped out onto the terrace that overlooked the gardens.

The Willstencraft house on the edge of Mayfair was one of the largest in London. It boasted three wings, with three floors each, and a full formal garden behind a high stone wall. The terrace ran the length of the center wing, with a set of central stairs leading down onto moonlit paths. Already several couples had succumbed to its quiet temptation, moving among the flowers, heads together. Alex refused to make himself an easy target. He led the girl a little way along the balustrade where they could be easily seen by anyone coming out of the house or looking up from the garden. He kept himself just close enough to converse, but not close enough to appear to be in contact with her. "Well?" he asked.

He could see her swallow in the moonlight. "This is more difficult than I thought. How does Katherine manage so well?"

"Your stepsister is a remarkable woman," he replied, struggling to be patient. "Determined and brave. I would suggest you find a similar courage. If our absence is noticed, your reputation could be damaged."

"My reputation is not the issue. What is far more important to me is my stepsister's happiness."

He frowned. "Is something endangering that?"

"Most assuredly. Me."

"You?"

"Oh, not on purpose," she told him. "I would never do anything to hurt Katherine. She has been my friend, my advisor, my comforter. I always thought I would do anything for her. In Deuteronomy it says to be strong and of good courage, but I find my courage lacking when Katherine needs me most."

He crossed his arms over his chest. "So, she *did* put you up to this."

"No, no, you mistake me! But you are right that Katherine hopes we will wed."

"Miss Templeman," he said as gently as he could, "I have told your stepsister and now I tell you—I am not interested in courting."

"Courting at all, or simply courting me?"

She was regarding him fixedly, and he felt his color rising. "That, madam, is none of your affair."

"But it is!" she insisted. "I must know. Katherine so has her heart set on it."

"Katherine will have to resign herself to disappointment. Let me return you to your admirers."

"No, wait, please." The tears were falling. He could see darker dots sprinkling the bosom of her gown. He pulled a handkerchief from his coat pocket and handed it to her with a sigh. She dabbed at her eyes, sniffing.

"I am sorry, my lord, but this is so important to me."

"I understand. Miss Collins has explained to me about your cousin and your father's fortune."

Her eyes were luminous. "She did?"

"Yes." Despite himself, he felt his righteous anger failing. She was a taking little thing. "I am very sorry for your situation, Miss Templeman. And I understand you have your heart set on me. Miss Collins seems to think I am the perfect candidate."

"Oh, but you are," she agreed fervently.

He smiled. "Thank you, my dear. But I am assured you will find some other fellow equally impressive."

"Never," she swore, sniffing again. "You are absolutely ideal."

"You honor me," he demurred.

"Not at all. What woman would refuse a gentleman so handsome, so charming. You are intelligent, well liked, well established."

"Your regard is flattering, Miss Templeman, but I fear I must stand by my principles. I cannot marry you."

"Marry me?" She stopped sniffing to stare at him. "Why would I wish to marry you, Lord Borin?"

He blinked. "Pardon me. I could have sworn you just said as much."

She shook her head. "I certainly did not. I promise you I have no interest in having you court me. I wish you to court my stepsister. It is apparent to me that Katherine is quite smitten with you."

He grinned, then immediately sobered. Now why did his heart leap at the idea? He had called Katherine a remarkable woman. Did it therefore follow that he was intrigued enough to court her? Or that she truly wished it?

"I am not certain how you reached that conclusion," he said carefully, "or that it is valid. However, supposing that it is, I do not see how that changes matters. I am not in the petticoat line, Miss Templeman. I have other matters to attend to at the moment."

She sighed, a sound as dejected as the slump of her shoulders. "Then nothing I can say will encourage you to continue your attentions to my sister?"

"Nothing I can think of at the moment." He paused as she sniffed again. "But as much as you have been circulating among the *ton,* perhaps you can help me with my task. Tell me, Miss Templeman. What do you know of these rumors about a spy among us?"

"A spy?" Her eyes widened in her tear-streaked face. "Someone is spying? Do you suspect Katherine?"

He started. In truth, he had not truly considered a woman the target of the foreign agent simply because few were admitted to the War Office. But husbands spoke to wives and men to their mistresses. Why not a woman? And if he had to pick a woman with a heart for intrigue, he could think of no one finer than Katherine Collins.

Yet as quickly as he seized on the idea, he dropped it. She could not be the spy. For one thing, he did not think she knew enough of the right people to gain access to information, and for another, he could not see her betraying her country. She might need money, but somehow he knew she would not trade military secrets to earn it.

"No, Miss Templeman," he answered her, "I cannot suspect your stepsister. And your response tells me you know nothing as well. Do not let the matter concern you. The War Office is well aware of the matter. I am certain the villain will be caught."

"A shame Katherine could not help you," she replied with a smile. She wiped away the last of her tears and held out the sodden handkerchief.

"I agree," he replied, gingerly accepting it from her and managing to stuff it into his coat pocket. "Miss Collins is endlessly resourceful. She would make an excellent addition to the Secret Service. Now let us return before anyone notices our absence."

She nodded. "Yes, of course. I have never done this—slipped away with a gentleman. Perhaps I should go in first and you should follow later?"

He smiled at her attempt at intrigue. "A wise precaution. Try to enjoy the rest of the ball, my dear. Your stepsister seems to have more than her share of admirers. Perhaps one of them will prove worthy."

She gave him a watery smile and hurried back to the door to the house.

He stood on the terrace, thinking. Would it really be such a hardship to court Miss Collins? She interested him more than any woman had done. The feelings he had for her could very well blossom into love. But was it fair to enter into any courtship when a part of him still hoped to join Lord Hastings's forces? He couldn't see his sprite being happy with the half-truths he'd be allowed to tell her. More likely she'd want to be part of the game. And he did not think he could work knowing his wife was exposed to danger. Best to simply stick to his course.

If he could stick to it. When he thought about it, he was disgusted by how easily he was distracted. First the intriguing Miss Collins, then her stepsister, and now the prospect of marriage. If he had any sense, he would return to the ball and demand that Hastings let him in on the game.

He moved toward the door, only to have it open in his face. Lord Templeman glared at him.

"I hope you won't make me call you out over my cousin, Borin," he growled.

Alex merely eyed him. "What a singularly stupid suggestion, Templeman. What would possess you to attempt suicide when you could wait a few more weeks and have the fortune with no trouble?"

"Ha!" Templeman crowded forward, forcing Alex back. "Then you *are* after the money!"

"I could care less about Miss Templeman's fortune, or lack thereof," Alex informed him. "You have no reason to accost me. Take yourself off."

"Not until I am certain you have no interest in my cousin."

"What do you all want from me?" Alex demanded. "Shall I post an ad in *The Times?* 'Lord Borin tenderly regrets that he has absolutely no interest in courting the fair Miss Templeman.' There are far more likely candidates in the ballroom. Go accost one of them."

"But you are the only one she took to the terrace." He smirked, making his unpleasant face even more so. "I saw her return, Borin. She'd been crying."

"Which any reasonable man would see as a sign that I had diminished myself in her affections." He moved to pass the rudesby, but Templeman caught his arm.

"Or dallied with her affections," he challenged. "Are you the type of man to offer for a girl you've compromised?"

"No, I'm the type to slit her encroaching relative's blasted throat. Now take your hands off me."

Some of his anger must have shown in his face, for Templeman dropped his hold. His eyes narrowed craftily. "I could make it worth your while to walk away."

Alex stared at him, stomach roiling. Miss Collins had not overstated the case when she made him out to be a villain. Templeman must have taken his disgusted silence as interest, for his little eyes widened in obvious glee.

"Yes, indeed, my lord. I can help you in any number of ways. I have connections, here and abroad. Do you like French champagne? The blockade will not stop my agents. Do you prefer Spanish gold? I have a chest. Arabian horses? I know where they are foaled. Tell me what you want, and I will get it for you."

"You have nothing to offer me," Alex replied, yanking himself free. The very idea of taking anything from the fellow made his skin crawl. He started to go, then paused. French champagne? Spanish gold? Arabian horses? Could Templeman be connected to the foreign agent? He stared at the porcine face, where even now a fine sweat was beading. Surely even foreign agents had higher standards for their operatives.

"You thought of something," Templeman accused as if he could see inside Alex's head. "I must have something of advantage to you. Say the word, my lord. Your desires are but music to my ears."

Alex blinked. "Music? Of course."

Templeman moved closer. "Yes?"

How very perfect. He could do one last good deed for Miss Collins, to show her and her stepsister he bore them no ill will. "There is one thing you can do for me," he told Templeman. "Grant this request, and I promise you I will never offer for your cousin."

Templeman eyed him suspiciously. "What?"

"You have something that belongs to Miss Collins. Return her harp and any materials that go with it, and I will cease my suit of Miss Templeman."

He frowned. "The harp? Why should you care whether Miss Collins has her harp?"

"That should not concern you. My price is a small one. Would you prefer I make it larger?"

He held up his hands. "No, no. The harp it shall be. Do I have your word as a gentleman, then?" He stuck out his hand.

Alex eyed the meaty fingers but refused to take them. Templeman slowly withdrew his hand.

"My word as a gentleman," Alex said solemnly. "When I have seen the harp returned, I will stop courting Miss Templeman. But not one second sooner."

Thirteen

Katherine had noticed when Lord Borin and Constance slipped out to the terrace together. Throughout the ball, she had, of course, alternated between watching her stepsister and watching him. She saw the exact moment when they came together, the looks that passed between them, the closeness of their heads as they conversed.

She told herself she should be pleased. Her stepsister had at last exerted her charms, and, as Katherine had predicted, Lord Borin was no match against them. That they remained outside for so long must mean he was offering for her. She could imagine him speaking words of love. He would be poetic and profound—no trite phrases for Alexander Wescott. And Constance would murmur agreement, and then they would kiss, lips melding in a promise for the future.

She groaned aloud, causing her partner to eye her with concern. Face flaming, she barely managed to finish the dance, then, pleading fatigue, she drove off her hoard of followers. She lowered her face to hide her telltale cheeks and moved to a different vantage point where she could watch the doors to the terrace.

What was wrong with her? This was what she had hoped for. She had planned and worked and schemed for Lord Borin to offer. She should rejoice. Unfortunately, her heart felt like lead in her breast and she was very much afraid she would burst into tears at any moment. No doubt it was merely the tension of seeing her goals finally achieved.

She had to fend off requests for her hand for another dance before she saw the doors open and Constance slip back inside. But even at this distance she could see something was wrong. Her stepsister's shoulders were slumped, and as she hurried closer, Katherine could see that Constance had been crying. Her heart sank. Had she refused him after all? Katherine motioned her stepsister to her and huddled with her against the Chinese-patterned wallpaper.

"What happened?" she pressed. "Are you all right?"

Constance gave her a weak smile. "I shall endure. But if we are going to survive this night, I had better make use of the lady's retiring room."

Katherine agreed, and they hurried to the room down the corridor that their hostess had set up for the ladies. They could not speak freely there as other women were in evidence, but they pretended to be overheated from the dancing and splashed cool water from a gilded basin onto Constance's cheeks. With any luck, the drying dots of moisture on her gown would be taken as perspiration from dancing. When Katherine was reasonably certain no one else would think her stepsister had been crying, she drew her out of the room.

"Lord Borin could not have caused this," she whispered as they found a quiet corner of the ballroom in which to converse.

"No," Constance agreed. "It was my own fault. I tried to be brave like you, Katherine, but I fear I lack your fortitude."

Katherine felt herself pale. What had happened on that terrace? "Brave like me? What are you talking about?"

Constance sighed. "I suppose it does not matter now whether I confess my feelings or not. I asked Lord Borin if he was courting and he indicated he was not interested."

Katherine squeezed her hand. "Oh, my poor dear. When I saw the two of you go out, I thought perhaps he had changed his mind. Are you terribly crushed?"

"Just disappointed. I had so hoped you would make a match of it."

She stared at her. "Me? You spoke to him about me?"

Constance nodded. "Yes. Forgive me. It just seemed you were so taken with him. And I rather thought he was taken with you."

Now she knew her cheeks were blazing. "What could possibly give you that impression?"

"The way he smiled when you walked into the room. The way his eyes were drawn to you, followed you, watched you. It seemed to me the mark of a man besotted."

"No," Katherine replied with a sigh. "It was more likely the mark of a man suspicious, and with good reason. I think that if Lord Borin truly knew me, he would find me far too managing a female to interest him. Besides, if he could not love you, what chance could I have?"

"I think you judge yourself too harshly," Constance murmured. "There are many kinds of beauty, Katherine, some more obvious than others."

"And men are inevitably drawn to the obvious sort." She shook her head. "Do not pity me, Constance. Like you, I shall endure. But what about you? Can you stand to attend the rest of the ball after this?"

"I must. I would not wish tongues to wag. Besides, if I leave, you must do so as well, and I do not want Lord Borin to think you are pining away for him."

"Good for you. Perhaps we should take note of just what Lord Borin *is* thinking." She glanced about the room to see what had become of their quarry but found him absent. Just as she frowned, she spotted him entering the room from the terrace.

Right behind Lord Templeman.

"Why would those two be together?" she wondered aloud.

Constance had obviously followed her gaze, for she sucked in a breath. "My cousin and Lord Borin? I cannot imagine an unlikelier pair."

Neither could Katherine. That Templeman might attempt to harass the viscount again was more than the outside of enough. She had to put a stop to the man's machinations. She started forward. "Stay here, Constance. I intend to get to the bottom of this."

"Wait!" Constance cried, reaching out to halt. "What will you do? I thought we agreed it was best to stay away from Lord Borin, pretend nothing happened."

"We agreed you would so pretend. I intend to learn his business with Lord Templeman. If your cousin has frightened him away, I think I shall spoil Lady Willstencraft's ball and have a proper fit."

Constance's eyes were huge, but she let go. The way she bit her lip, however, told Katherine she had grave misgivings.

Katherine wasn't entirely sanguine about the matter herself, but if Lord Templeman was somehow behind the viscount's refusal, she had to stop him. Beyond her, she heard the musicians start up another dance. She stepped up to the viscount and smiled sweetly.

"I am so glad you returned in time for the dance you promised me, Lord Borin. Shall we?"

He stared at her for a moment, and she couldn't help but wonder what he was thinking. Unfortunately, he seemed to have gotten better at hiding his feelings. The slight frown of his golden brows could have meant anything from confusion to annoyance. At last he bowed and offered her his arm to take her out on the floor.

She had hoped there might be an uneven number of couples so that they would be forced to stand out at the top and bottom of the set. If they were not needed by the pattern of the dance, they might have a moment for more private conversation and she would not have to resort to tricking him onto the terrace. Unfortunately, not only was the number of couples even, but the dance was "Hole in the Wall," one of the more active ones. She was constantly crossing and circling and stepping about, leaving no time for privacy.

It did, however, leave the viscount with plenty of time to observe her, and she was not a little unnerved by the warm caress of his gaze. When he surreptitiously squeezed her hand in passing, she blushed, and when he winked as he crossed to her side, she had to school her face lest her grin give him away.

As the dance ended, he bowed. "Thank you, Miss Collins, for a most enjoyable dance. I would ask for another, but I fear my reputation would not bear it."

"Your reputation?" She shook her head with a smile. "I was under the impression that it was the lady's reputation that must be guarded."

"Not at all. A gentleman prides himself on a reputation of honor." His smile faded, and she watched as his gaze sought out Lord Templeman across the room. So, something had happened between the two. Determined to learn what, she laid a hand on his arm.

"I must speak to you, alone."

His gaze returned to her, curiosity mixed with annoyance. "You, too? I suppose I should not be surprised. Is this absolutely necessary, Miss Collins?"

"Yes. Please?"

She had not intended the word to sound so desperate, but he was obviously not proof against it. He let out a sigh of resignation. With a curt nod, he led her on a promenade. It was the work of a moment to pull him out the door.

"Ah, the terrace," he said. "How very original. I wonder if it has changed since I last saw it only a few short moments ago."

"Stop it," she scolded. "It was because you were out here that I must talk to you."

He sighed. "I assure you your stepsister's reputation will not suffer. She can tell you I was a gentleman."

"Of course you were. It is not in you to behave reprehensibly."

He blinked. "Thank you, I think. But if you knew that, then why this subterfuge?"

"I saw you come in with Lord Templeman. Did he threaten you?"

He raised a brow. "Your care for my tender feelings overwhelms me, but I assure you I am able to defend myself against the likes of Templeman."

Katherine sighed. "I did not want to put you in the position where you had to defend yourself."

"Then you should not have connected me with your stepsister, for Templeman will threaten anyone who tries to separate him from that fortune."

"Was he so blatant as to say that? His wickedness grows."

The door opened to admit a tall dark-haired gentleman, consummate in his evening black. The viscount turned as if to hide his face and took her arm. Sure he meant to protect her reputation, she allowed him to lead her down the terrace toward the steps to the garden. He did not mention the incident, however, simply continuing with their conversation.

"Yes, I fear Lord Templeman does grow more bold," he said as they walked arm in arm down the stairs. "You would do well to keep away from him, my dear."

"Your care for my tender feelings overwhelms me, my lord," she quipped, forcing herself not to look back to see if the tall gentleman was watching. "But I refuse to let Constance lose her fortune without a fight."

"Somehow, I thought you would say that."

She heard the resignation in his tone. She tried to focus on the garden around them. A few early roses drowsed in the moonlight, their perfume caressing the cool air. She could hear the murmur of voices to their left and right. Other couples walked in the fragrant evening. Somehow she thought their activities were less onerous than hers. "I will not do you the disservice of petitioning for your help again," she said. "But would you at least tell me his strategy so that I might thwart him in the future?"

He lifted up a particularly heavy bower for her to cross under it. She ducked under his arm and felt it settle naturally about her shoulders. She stiffened, but his conversation continued as unhurried as his steps. "I would be delighted to outline his nasty campaign. He starts by bullying with his consequence, moves to physical threats, and ends with bribery."

Only the last surprised her. "Bribery? With what could he possibly bribe you?"

Glancing up over her shoulder, she saw him smile. "In truth, very little. You could find far more interesting things."

"Really?" She frowned. "Such as?"

He stopped to gaze down at her. The breeze ruffled

his hair, made silver by the moon. "As you have such a high opinion of me as a gentleman, Miss Collins, I shall have to refrain from answering that question."

She gazed up at him, captivated by the heat from eyes that should have been as cool as the night sky above them. He leaned closer, his breath a caress on her cheek.

"You should return to the ballroom now, my dear."

"Should I?" She could not seem to move her feet. Indeed, her entire body seemed to be enveloped in a luscious lassitude.

"Indeed," he murmured. "I walked away from our kiss last time. If you are so unwise as to let me kiss you again now, I am not certain either of us will walk away."

Her heart hammered a warning. She refused to be bullied. "Like you, I am not impressed by threats, my lord."

"Pity," he murmured as his mouth descended on hers.

But it was nothing like being bullied. His lips were warm and gentle against hers, the pressure building a pleasurable tension through her. Desire coiled around her limbs, forced her arms up about his neck, urged her to press against him, to hold him close. If this was seduction, she only wanted more.

Somewhere nearby a woman giggled. Katherine broke away from him with a gasp. Her gaze darted about, but she saw no one else among the bushes. His smile lazy, he moved to take her in his arms again.

"Stop, please." Her breathlessness was evident, and she took a deep gulp of air to sustain herself. "I will give you a disgust of me if I let this continue."

"I promise you nothing about you disgusts me," he murmured, but he did not continue his advance.

"Easily won is little valued," she retorted. "I took

you for a gentleman, my lord." She stepped purposely out of his reach. The night seemed suddenly colder.

He stiffened, then bowed. "Forgive me, Miss Collins. My behavior with you has been unconscionable. However, I did warn you."

"So you did. To think I did not heed the warning. I shall in the future, I promise you."

He bowed again. "I can only beg your pardon."

She felt a hysterical laugh bubbling up. "Bit late for that, my lord. Be thankful I had not set out to trap you into marriage, for if I had, you would be mine now."

He straightened, moonlight haloing the gold of his hair. "If you wish me to speak to your guardian, of course I shall."

She shook her head. "Don't be ridiculous. I understand you were simply flirting."

Some part of her wished him to gainsay her, promising complete devotion for an eternity. She was not entirely surprised, however, when he agreed with her that he was only playing.

"I am glad you understand, but I should not have kissed you. Your reputation . . ."

"Is perfectly safe," she assured him, wrapping her heart in regrets and tucking it neatly away. "As is yours. I trust we can count on each other to keep this meeting private."

"Of course," he replied. "I apologize again, Miss Collins. I hope you will not refine on my behavior."

"Not at all," Katherine said, far more blithely than she thought she would be able. "I thank you for the kiss, my lord. It was delightful. But do not think I put any weight behind it. I will return to the ball now. Do not trouble yourself further."

Fourteen

Alex told himself to remember those words. There was nothing in the fascinating Miss Collins's kiss to trouble him. Unfortunately there was everything in his own reaction. He could not deny her attraction. The touch of her lips raised a fire in him that was not easily extinguished. He had spoken the truth—he had not wanted to walk away, to let her out of his arms. Yet he had done just that. Being a gentleman was at times a blasted inconvenience!

The best thing he could do was to let the Collinses go their way before he was tempted further. But first he had to be certain Templeman lived up to his word.

He wasn't sure whether to be gratified or disappointed that he saw no one follow him home from the ball. Neither did he see anyone as he moved about his activities the next day. Unfortunately, whatever he did, he could not put Miss Collins out of his mind.

Though he still hoped to find a way to convince Lord Hastings to change his mind, he had no other leads on his mysterious pursuers. The only indication that Lord Hastings might be taking the pursuit more seriously had been the interference of Trevithan at the ball. His lordship's man had been rather blatant about poking his head out onto the terrace while Alex was with Miss Collins. He had not followed them into the garden. That might have indicated that the fellow was a gentleman, or that Alex wasn't worth his valuable time. Either way, Alex could see no reason not to carry on with his regular routine.

He started with some exercise at Gentleman Jackson's. In the middle of a bout with Kevin Whattling he paused to think that his sprite would enjoy attending the next prize fight with him and nearly had his head taken off by Whattling's punishing right.

He retreated to his tailor's to be measured for a new coat. With one arm raised, he caught himself wondering whether Miss Collins would like the cut of it and had to be told twice to lower his arm so the tailor's assistant could continue working.

He then tried inspecting the horses at Tattersall's for a new mount, only to be distracted by a spirited mare that he thought would be perfect for Miss Collins. The coat was the same color as her eyes.

He was clearly lost.

In desperation, he repaired to White's. A quick check of the betting books only depressed him further. Some industrious chap had wagered a quid that Alex would marry Miss Templeman before the Season was out. Alex wanted to add a note about the intelligence of the fellow, but he supposed it wasn't sporting to compare him to a door handle. After all, he maligned the handle.

He slouched in a wing chair in the corner of the club and tried to convince himself that he could spend the rest of his life without thinking of the adorable Miss Collins. Despite what he was sure was a gloomy appearance, several cronies attempted to join him. They should have been a marvelous distraction, but today he couldn't seem to enjoy their witty conversation. He caught himself wondering if any of them would care if he simply disappeared off the face of the earth. Certainly none of his acquaintances, except perhaps the kindhearted, ever-helpful Giles Sloan, would go to the trouble Katherine Collins had to ensure her stepsister's welfare.

He had managed to scare all his friends away at last when an attendant brought him word from Lord Templeman.

"The exact statement his man gave was 'it is done.' Does this have some meaning to you, my lord?"

Assuring the fellow that it did, he hurried for the Collins house to confirm the news.

Bixby met him at the door. He wasn't entirely sure of his reception, but the butler actually went so far as to wink at him in greeting. Alex smiled back, then followed him to the familiar withdrawing room.

Standing in the corner was an elegant maple harp, the rose-tinted wood varnished to a high sheen. The graceful curve and pillar were decorated with scrolls, like the top of a Grecian column. The strings gleamed in the light from the windows. Emma was just finishing polishing it, and Miss Collins stood beside her in a pool of sunlight, inspecting her work. The glow made a ruddy halo about her auburn hair. He barely noticed as Miss Templeman rose from her spot on the settee to greet him.

"Have I come at an inconvenient time?" he asked.

His sprite and the plump housekeeper turned to him immediately. His heart leaped at the pleasure in the young lady's gaze, but she lowered her head as if to hide the look from him. He felt a pang of guilt. Had she not forgiven him for the interlude in the garden after all?

Miss Templeman was more welcoming. "There can never be a bad time for you to visit, Lord Borin," she assured him, moving to his side to catch up his hands and pull him toward the instrument. Her green-sprigged muslin gown swirled about her legs. "Look what came today! Katherine has her harp back."

Their gray-haired housekeeper gathered her things to leave, giving Alex a quick smile before departing. His sprite kept her head lowered.

"A lovely instrument, to be sure," he replied, eyeing her for a response. "Almost as lovely as its owner."

Two spots of color appeared on her cheeks. She turned to run a hand down the curve of the frame, the movement a lingering caress that boded no good for his honorable intentions.

"I cannot believe it is returned to me," she murmured. "I suspect you may have had a hand in this, Lord Borin."

"Now, why would you suspect that?" he asked with a smile.

She raised her head to eye him, curiosity evident in that gray gaze. "Could this favor be part of your discussion with Lord Templeman?"

Her stepsister was eying him as well. He ignored the question. "Let us not spend time in subterfuge today," he said. "Would you favor us with a song, Miss Collins?"

She shook her head, regretfully, he thought. "It has been ages since I played. I only just tuned it."

"Oh, Katherine, surely you haven't forgotten how to play," her stepsister chided. "At most you will be a little stiff. Lord Borin will not mind if you stumble a bit."

But she would mind. He could see it in her eyes. What was it she had said last night—she didn't wish to give him a disgust of her? In fact, she did not look willing to do anything that might put her in a less-than-perfect light. He wanted to assure her that there was nothing she could do that would change his respect for her, but they had an audience.

"Please, Miss Collins?" he urged. "It would mean a great deal to me."

"You may change your mind after you hear me," she replied. "But very well. If you two would take your seats."

As Alex and Constance sat on two of the blue velvet chairs nearby, she perched on the lion-footed stool behind the instrument. Alex watched as she peeled off her gloves and set them aside. Carefully arranging her lavender skirts, she tipped the harp back until it rested against her shoulder. Alex had the feeling his head would nestle there just as nicely. She flexed her fingers and then poised them over the strings, elbow and thumb up, fingers curved, elegant. He could imagine those hands in such a position over his own body. He tried to focus on something else and found himself holding his breath, waiting for her to begin. Closing her eyes and nodding her head to a beat only she could hear, she began playing.

The melody flowed from the instrument like a brook tumbling over pebbles in the spring. The sound swept over him, enveloped him, pulled him along. He thought that if he closed his eyes, he might float away on the sound. But he could not turn his gaze from the rapt expression on Miss Collins's face. The music purged all tension, all concerns, from her. She glowed with a happiness and peace he was sure few mortals possessed. It was as if she had exposed her soul, and it was so glorious a thing as to humble him.

When the last note died away, she met his gaze and a tear trickled down one cheek. "Thank you, my lord," she murmured. "I did not realize how much I missed that."

He could not answer her. He swallowed the lump in his throat and merely nodded.

"Oh, Katherine, that was lovely," her stepsister said

beside him, wiping a tear from her own eye. "It took me right back to Sunday afternoons with Father. How he loved to hear you play."

"How I loved to play for him," she replied with a sad smile. "He had a way of listening that made me want to play my best for him."

"Not unlike the way Lord Borin listens," Miss Templeman said with a smile to him.

His sprite blushed. "Yes, quite like that."

He felt warmed by her praise. "Thank you, both. I am honored if my presence contributed to that lovely song. You have great talent, Miss Collins."

Her blush deepened. "Thank you, my lord."

There was a commotion by the door, and her brother catapulted into the room, Sir Richard at his heels.

"You see, Uncle," the boy proclaimed, "I told you I heard music. Katherine was playing."

"Yes, so it seems. Good afternoon, Borin. Come to admire the beauty?"

Alex suspected Sir Richard referred to the instrument rather than Alex's fascination with his niece, but Miss Collins spoke before he could answer. "Lord Borin appears to enjoy the music of the harp."

"A deaf man would enjoy music the way you play," her uncle replied with a wink to Alex.

Alex returned his smile. "I quite agree, sir."

Eric rushed forward to tug on her hand. "Play something else, Katherine."

"Not now, Eric." She put him back and rose as if to forestall further requests. "I must find my sheet music and practice first."

His face fell.

Sir Richard chuckled. "You'd do anything to get out of your studies, wouldn't you, scamp?"

"Sums," Eric confided to Alex, and rolled his blue eyes.

"A decided nuisance, to be sure," Alex replied, feeling his sprite's gaze on him. "But I have found them to come in handy from time to time. Best to simply get them over with."

Eric sighed. "I suppose." Then he brightened. "But as you're here, shouldn't we have some refreshment first? Katherine? Uncle?"

Alex watched as Miss Collins and Sir Richard exchanged glances, this time of amusement. He felt another pang, but knew it came from envy. He had never realized how lonely he'd been until seeing the Collinses together. Their support and enjoyment of each other, even in the little things, called to his heart.

Miss Collins agreed to refreshments and Miss Templeman took the boy in hand to go fetch them. Alex would have liked nothing better than to talk with Miss Collins, but Sir Richard eased himself into the chair her stepsister had vacated and Alex could not politely extricate himself. He sat and discussed the happenings on the Peninsula. He could not keep his eyes from straying to where his sprite was lovingly draping a dust cloth over her instrument. Her movements were graceful, her dark brow furrowed as if deep in thought. He wondered what she was thinking and had to recall himself sharply to the conversation when Sir Richard asked him a question.

He had not intended to spend so much time at the Collinses', but it was early evening before he took his leave. His heart was heavy as he realized he had no reason to call again. Indeed, should he continue to call, Templeman might take it in his head that Alex was continuing his suit. While he owed the man no favors, he had given his word, and he did not like to think how the fellow might torment Miss Templeman or Miss Collins. The best thing for all of them was for him to stay away.

His sprite seemed to sense it was the last time he would visit, for she insisted on walking him to the door herself.

"Thank you again for seeing that my harp was restored to me, my lord," she said. "I shall never forget your kindness." She stood on tiptoe and pressed a kiss against his cheek, soft and sweet. He was certain he would not have been able to stop himself from returning the kiss and far less chastely, if Bixby hadn't been waiting to throw open the door for him. As it was, he could do no more than take her hand.

She had evidently forgotten to replace her gloves, and he fancied he could feel the silk of her skin through his own. He bent and pressed a kiss against the back of her hand, breathing in the fresh scent of her. Her strong fingers tensed in his. On impulse, he turned her hand and pressed a second kiss more deeply into her palm. He heard her sharp intake of breath and knew she had been as affected as he was.

Rising, he offered her a smile. "Good-bye, Miss Collins. I wish you every happiness."

"Good-bye, Lord Borin," she murmured. "I wish you happy as well."

The butler opened the door with a snap. Alex could find no excuse to prolong his stay. He accepted his hat from Bixby, clapped it on his head, and strolled down the steps to the street. Anyone watching, he was sure, would only see a cultured gentleman on his way to an evening of entertainment.

But he rather thought his life would not be sufficiently entertaining ever again.

Katherine hurried to the library to watch him go. He would not return. There was no reason. He would not court Constance, and he should not court her. He had far more important things to do. He would join the war effort and distinguish himself. If she ever saw him again, he would have a chest full of medals, and likely a beautiful bride on his arm.

The tears were coming, and she blinked them back fiercely. In so doing, she nearly missed the movement across the street. A dark shadow detached itself from the neighbor's wall and slipped into place behind the viscount.

He was being followed.

She sucked in a breath. What should she do? He had accused her of not trusting his ability to manage his own affairs. Perhaps he knew of his shadow and simply led the creature into a trap. But he walked so calmly, as if he hadn't a care in the world. Was it just a ruse? She did not think him so skilled at subterfuge.

What if he didn't know? What if the creature were a footpad, out to rob him, or worse? What if even now he walked to his doom?

She fled into the entry. "Bixby!"

"Yes, Miss Katherine?" Her man materialized out of the dark of the stair.

"Someone's following Lord Borin. We must stop him."

He did not question her, merely nodding, but she saw the light spring to life in his eyes. "I'll go now."

"Wait." She snatched up her cloak from the hook beside the door. "Let me come with you."

"It's too dangerous," he chided. He shrugged out of the coat that would mark him for their servant, snatched up Sir Richard's cloak from the peg, and reached for the door.

"Entirely too dangerous," Sir Richard agreed, coming down the stair. Katherine squared her shoulders to fight, but he put a hand on her as if to hold her in place. He nodded to the butler, who slipped out the door. Katherine sagged in defeat.

Sir Richard let go of her to pat her arm. "Have a little faith, girl. I know the men in your life have been a disappointing lot, but Lord Borin is made of stronger stuff. He will be fine."

She nodded and let him lead her back to the withdrawing room. Eric and Constance were engaged in a game of ninepins. The rattle of the wooden pins against the polished board grated on her nerves. She wandered to the window and peered out into the dark night, trying to think of anything except the viscount. But everything reminded her of him. The sky overhead was a blue black as deep as his eyes. The breeze would be as soft as his breath on her cheek. The garden below was only a smaller version of the one in which they had walked, and talked, and kissed just the night before. She could not let him be harmed. She would never forgive herself if her schemes had led to this.

Bixby did not return until after a dinner Emma served and Katherine barely tasted. Then he called Sir Richard aside. Katherine hurried after them.

She could not help but notice that Bix looked weary. The light in his eyes was dimmed, and his mobile mouth was set in grim lines.

"I followed him home," he reported to them. "So did his shadow. I could have waited for his lordship, but I thought it better to try to learn more about our shadow. He waited at the house, but then another fellow joined him and the first left. I went with him, all the way until he went into an apartment house. Never did get a good look at the chap. I thought I better report rather than wait any longer."

Katherine found herself biting her lip and let it go with a sigh. "Then we do not know whether Lord Borin is safe."

Bixby shook his head, sending a chill through her. His next words caused the last of her warmth to flee.

"There's something havey cavey going on, Miss Katherine. That spy I followed? He went home to roost at the same apartment house where I met Lord Borin's mistress."

Fifteen

Lord Templeman was pleased as he sat down to dinner that night. What had started as a beastly day had ended much happier.

It had been lowering to return Miss Collins's harp. Not that he had any use for the great ugly thing. Far from it. It was one more bit of useless gilt cluttering up his otherwise impressive town house. The only reason he had held it this long was that it gave him great enjoyment to torment, even in small ways, those who kept him from his rightful fortune.

Whoever heard of separating the money from the title? He was Lord Templeman now; he had a duty to live up to his increased consequence. From the moment he had realized as a youth that the only thing that stood between him and the title was his weak uncle, he had patiently waited his turn. How he'd sweated when Constance's mother had been pregnant. How pleased he'd been that the woman had not only birthed a girl child but thoughtfully died shortly thereafter.

He had done all he could to keep his uncle single. He had never known what magic Miss Katherine Collins had woven when a music recital featuring her on a friend's harp had brought her widowed mother and his uncle together. But at least any concerns of additional children were past at last. Now he just had to take the fortune from Constance. What did two chits straight from the schoolroom, a whey-faced boy, and a cripple know about handling money anyway? It was far better off in his hands.

And then there was Borin, who liked to think of himself as a great gentleman. Gentleman, ha! Templeman had seen how he looked at Miss Collins. Borin might be courting Constance's fortune, but he lusted after the stepsister. Rather strange that. Templeman liked his women quiet, experienced, and substantial, but any idiot could see that in the Collins house, Constance was the greater beauty. Lord Borin obviously had different tastes.

But he didn't much care what the man did with his eccentricities so long as he did not threaten the fortune. Templeman had returned the blasted harp, for all the good it had done him. There was Borin, back taking refreshments, neat as you please. The fellow had stayed longer than ever, or so Templeman's runner relayed.

Well, two could play at this game. If Borin did not feel honor bound to keep his word, neither did Templeman. The battle lines had been drawn, and Templeman had no doubt he would be the winner for the simple reason that he had no intention of fighting fairly.

He had two factors in his favor. No one seemed to suspect him behind the spy rumors, yet everyone was mad to learn more. And he had several fine Indian rubies in his possession with which to entice a certain ladybird to sing.

Somehow he thought her music would be far more interesting than anything Miss Collins could play on her harp.

* * *

Sir Richard was far less pleased by the course of the day's events. He could not remember Katherine being so upset as she had been when learning that Borin might be in danger. He had had to threaten the girl with bodily harm to keep her from going to Borin right then. It was quite clear to him that she had fallen in love with the fellow.

Unfortunately, from Borin's manner that day, Sir Richard also had a strong suspicion that the young lord did not intend to renew the acquaintance. He did not understand why. Borin was interested, perhaps more than interested. Yet he refused to commit. His niece was doomed to heartache, he feared, if he did not find a way to intervene.

Even worse, however, was that Borin seemed to have blundered into something larger. Why else would he be shadowed? Common footpads would not have been after him for days on end without acting. He still thought it was more likely connected with this foreign agent business, though he doubted Borin realized it.

And what was the connection with Miss Montgomery, the actress? He'd been more than a little shocked to discover his niece was acquainted with Borin's last mistress. The looks exchanged between Katherine and Bixby told him it was more than mere knowledge through gossip. He decided not to ask the specific circumstances.

He did, however, decide there was someone he needed to consult. Accordingly, he made his way before noon the next day to the War Office, going quietly by way of a private entrance known only to a privileged few.

The Marquis of Hastings received him readily, coming around his desk to shake Richard's hand.

"Richard, good to see you again. To what do I owe this unexpected pleasure?"

Richard eased himself into the chair before the desk. If the marquis noted his difficulty as he took his own seat, he did not betray it and Richard liked him all the more for it.

"I have reason to believe," he told the marquis, "that a certain gentleman courting one of my wards is being followed. I wish to be certain you are not behind it."

His former supervisor made a show of polishing his timepiece against the silk of his navy striped waistcoat. "You think the fellow connected with the Service?"

"I know he would like to join your agency."

Hastings pocketed the watch as he blew out a breath. "Borin. Have no concern, Richard. I have known him for years; he went to school with my son. He would make a fine husband for either of your girls."

Despite himself, Richard felt disappointed. It would not be so easy after all. "Then you are not following him?"

Hastings shook his head. "No, but I am aware of the supposed incidents. Complained to you, did he?"

"Not in the slightest," Richard assured him. "He merely expressed a desire to discover the culprit. And these are not 'supposed' incidents, old man. I saw it happen. I had Bixby follow the pair of them last night."

Another person would not have seen the interest flair to life in Hastings's dark eyes. Richard strove to remain as cool as his former supervisor.

"And how is Bixby these days?" Hastings asked politely. "Still not ready to retire, I see."

"Not at all," Richard assured him, smoothing his brown coat over his tweed vest. "And I do believe he has infected my niece, Katherine, with his love for intrigue."

"How interesting. And did he find anything noteworthy on his reconnaissance last night?"

Richard had him now. "Only that the fellow following Borin was last seen entering the apartment house of Miss Lydia Montgomery."

The light faded from his eyes, and Hastings glanced at the papers on his desk. "Well, there you have it, then. Miss Montgomery merely wishes to be certain she still has a hold on Lord Borin's affections."

Richard clucked his tongue. "You are behind on the gossip, old fellow. Borin cast her off days ago. She has already switched allegiance to Rehmouth."

Hastings raised his gaze with a frown. "Indeed. You appear to be well informed as to Lord Borin's activities."

"I told you," Richard replied with a shrug, "he courts one of my wards."

"So you are being cautious. What do you suspect him of?"

Richard rose, pleased that he was able to do so without betraying the pain it caused. "I had thought you might suspect him of this spying business. However, as you are obviously not having him followed, I will have to investigate matters myself."

Hastings leaned back in his chair. "I could not have assigned a better man."

His former supervisor had never been given to sarcasm, so Richard decided to accept the compliment at face value. "Thank you. I ask only one thing in return. If I discover a connection to this spying business, I will let you know immediately. If you suspect Borin of misdeeds, I hope you will grant me the same courtesy."

"Agreed," Hastings replied with a nod. "And Richard, good luck, for all our sakes."

Katherine was not a little surprised to find her uncle up and gone when she went to call him late that morn-

ing. Neither Bixby nor Emma was aware he had left
either. She would have panicked if she hadn't found
The Morning Chronicle still folded on the breakfast
table as if it had never been read.

She was not sure what to make of it, but even that
mystery could not completely take her mind off the
viscount. Her uncle had made her promise not to interfere, and she could only hope he was out doing
something useful, such as alerting Bow Street. She
could not even focus on tutoring her brother. Finally,
she enlisted Constance to work with Eric and gave herself up to a couple of hours on her harp. She was
draping the instrument when Bixby appeared in the
doorway. His lean face was so stern that Katherine
could only frown. "What is it?"

"There's a person here to see Miss Constance. She
came heavily veiled and refused to give her name, but
I know that voice. It's Miss Montgomery."

"Lord Borin's mistress?" Katherine gathered up her
navy skirts to cross to his side. "Why would she want
to see Constance? Do you think she knows we sent
the ruby?"

Bixby's look darkened further. "I don't know, but I
cannot like her boldness in coming here."

Neither could Katherine. "Did she recognize you?"

He shook his head. "She'd have little cause. I spoke
to her maid when I delivered the ruby."

So much for that, then. "Where is she now?"

"I wanted to leave her to cool her heels on the front
step, but I didn't like to think what the neighbors would
say. I put her in the library. Shall I tell her Constance
is unavailable?"

"No." Katherine stood taller. "I will meet her. I
must learn why she came, particularly after last night's
episode. Warn Emma to keep the others away, then
join me."

The plan agreed upon, she hurried down to the library.

Miss Montgomery was standing as if perusing the shelves as Katherine entered. She could not have been seeing much, for she still wore the veiled bonnet. Her pelisse was a modest gray, but of such a fine material as to make Katherine feel downright dowdy in her simple navy day dress.

As Katherine moved toward her, her head turned. "You are not Miss Templeman." Her voice came out clearly despite her disguise, and she did not sound pleased.

"Miss Templeman is unavailable," Katherine replied. "I am the mistress of the house, Miss Collins." As soon as the words left her mouth she could feel herself blush. Perhaps it was the word "mistress."

Now the actress did sound amused. "How thoughtful of you to meet with me, Miss Collins. However, if Miss Templeman is unavailable, I believe my message should be left with older ears. Have you a guardian about somewhere?"

"Sir Richard Collins, my uncle, is also unavailable," Katherine told her, more annoyed than curious. "You will have to make do with me."

"Very well, then, if you insist. I simply wished to impart a word of warning about a certain gentleman who is persistent in his attentions to Miss Templeman. He is a vicious brute, and she would be well advised to stay away from him."

"How very thoughtful of you to be concerned about my stepsister's welfare," Katherine replied, mind whirling. She could not mean Lord Borin. "But perhaps if I knew your identity, I would be better able to evaluate the import of this message."

She stood a little taller. "My identity is immaterial.

Consider me a lost soul who seeks for others to avoid her fate."

That was certainly poetic. Katherine wondered if she had steady employment as an actress with such melodramatic lines. "Commendable, to be sure," she said. "However, my stepsister has so many admirers that if you do not provide me with the name of at least the gentleman, I cannot be sure whom you mean."

Her voice took on the timbre of a prophetess. "I speak of a wealthy gentleman, a titled gentleman, one you allow in your home for protracted periods."

Katherine could not resist baiting her. "Oh," she said wisely, "Lord Templeman. Well, have no fear. He does not court my stepsister. She has the misfortune to be related to him."

"My condolences," she snapped. Then, as if remembering herself, she resumed her oracles. "But I do not mean Lord Templeman. I refer to a handsome gentleman, one who could talk the birds from the trees with his gilded tongue and charming manner."

Katherine shrugged. "Sorry. All my stepsister's beaus seem charming. You cannot expect me to turn them all away."

Behind her she heard the door open and saw Bixby slide quietly into place along the wall. Miss Montgomery ignored him, voice rising.

"But this one has eyes as dangerous as his temper, dark as the sky before a thunderstorm."

"I do not notice eyes much. Could you be more specific?"

"Borin!" she snapped, throwing up her hands.

"Boring?" Katherine frowned to keep from laughing at the glee on Bixby's face. "Oh, well, yes, I fear it is quite tedious chaperoning my stepsister with one fellow after another, but what can one do?"

"Not boring you dim-witted shrew," Miss Montgomery nearly shouted. "Borin, Lord Borin. Viscount Borin, Alexander Wescott."

"Ohhhh," Katherine replied knowingly, catching a wink from Bixby. "Lord Borin. You must be mistaken. He isn't courting Miss Templeman."

"He isn't?" She must have realized that her surprise was obvious, for she quickly continued. "Of course he is. Silly chit. I begin to think you know nothing about men."

"And I begin to think you know nothing about Lord Borin," Katherine countered. "Your story of his brutality won't wash. He has been nothing if not a gentleman."

"Of that I am certain," she purred. "His ways are winning as long as he gets what he wants. But refuse him . . ." She reached up and draped the veil over the top of her bonnet. Despite herself, Katherine gasped.

"Rather colorful, isn't it?" Miss Montgomery smiled grimly, turning her sculptured face so that the lamplight glowed on the purple-and-green bruise obscuring the left side. "Not the first he's given me, but I must say it's one of the showiest."

"You lie!" Katherine spat. "Lord Borin would never do such a thing!" She started forward, to do what, she wasn't sure, but Bixby moved to block her way. Her feelings must have been all over her face. She couldn't seem to care.

"Oh, Lord Borin would do this and more if his desires are thwarted." Miss Montgomery returned her veil to its former position. "You see why I felt I must warn you."

"I see only that you are a jealous tart," Katherine replied, shaking with anger. "You aren't worthy to walk beside him."

"And you are a very blind little girl who's in for a nasty tumble. Don't expect Borin to pick you up."

Bixby caught Katherine's shoulders as Miss Montgomery sailed to the door. With a warning glance to Katherine, he released her and hurried to let the woman out.

Katherine stood in the library, hands balled at her sides, emotions churning. How dare she malign the viscount that way! It was too horrible to bear to think someone might believe him capable of such violence. The woman must be stopped!

"She must be lying," she said to Bix as he returned.

"Of course she's lying." Bixby rubbed his chin thoughtfully. "I'd wager that bruise was nothing more than paint. If anyone had hit her hard enough to leave that mark, I'd also wager the Duke of Rehmouth would have a thing or two to say about it. You pegged her, miss—she heard the rumors that his lordship had thrown her over to marry Miss Constance and she came here out of jealousy. Pay her no never mind."

She would have liked to do just that, but her stomach churned as fast as her emotions. "How can I," she demanded, "when she is connected to the ones who follow Lord Borin?"

Before he could answer, she gasped. "Oh, Bix, I'm an idiot! I was so busy baiting her I never thought to ask the connection. We lost our opportunity to learn who follows Lord Borin!"

Sixteen

Bix tried to console her, but Katherine would have none of it.

"I'll call on her," she threatened, starting for the door. "Turnabout is fair play. Fetch me a carriage, Bix."

"If you'd started that command with 'I shall kill him,' you'd sound just like Sir Richard," the butler replied, moving no farther than her side. "You can't do it, Miss Katherine. How would you explain a visit to someone like her?"

"I shall go at night, then, in disguise."

Bix shook his head. "It won't suffice. Too many people visit her at night. You'd be spotted sure."

"She came here," Katherine protested.

"And she has less reputation to protect. Please, Miss Katherine, calm down and think."

She knew he was right, but she couldn't seem to still her agitation. To think she had let such an opportunity slip by. She had to find a way to gain it back.

From out in the entry came the sound of the door.

Bixby stiffened. "That will be Sir Richard. Perhaps he can talk sense into you." He hurried out.

With no choice but to wait, Katherine paced the library. Why had she gotten so upset as to forget her purpose? Surely no one who knew Lord Borin would believe that ridiculous tale. Surely the woman would not even be so foolish as to repeat it in public. Bixby had the right of it—the story was a taradiddle concocted to sour Constance on a romance that was no more real. As such, the tale had only the power Katherine was willing to give it. She must force herself to focus on what was important.

By the time her uncle limped into the library, she had calmed herself sufficiently to tell him about their visitor.

"And so I let her go without asking whether she had hired the men to follow Lord Borin," Katherine concluded.

"She's enough of a witch to do it," Bixby stated. "Lord Borin never hit her, but I hear tell she beats her maid for nothing more than turning down her bed the wrong way."

"That's beastly," Katherine said, wrinkling her nose. "Then you think she had Lord Borin followed because she was jealous? I thought she had a new protector."

Her uncle scowled at her. "I refuse to ask how you know all this, young lady. Suffice it to say you are not to demonstrate your knowledge before anyone outside this house. Do I make myself clear?"

Katherine drew herself up. "Certainly, Uncle, but you have not answered the question. Why would she have Lord Borin followed and make up that story about him as well?"

"Someone doesn't want Borin hanging about," Sir Richard guessed.

"Lord Templeman," Bixby offered. "He's the only one with an interest."

"But would he stoop to this?" Katherine pressed. "Can we be certain Lord Borin isn't being followed for some more nefarious purpose?"

Sir Richard shook his head. "Unfortunately, no." He went on to relate the discussion he'd had with Lord Hastings at the War Office. Katherine felt her concern arise anew.

"Then he may indeed be the target of this spy?"

Her uncle's handsome face was grave. "No doubt he'd make a good choice. He is well known to much of the *ton* and has connections to the War Office. If someone knew he had been refused by the Service, they might believe him bitter enough to sell out his country."

"He was refused?" Katherine drew herself up. "What idiot did that? He would succeed at whatever he set his hand to."

Sir Richard smiled. "No doubt, my dear. But I am certain Lord Hastings had particular criteria in mind when he refused Lord Borin. Our task now is to determine if our young friend is in any danger and make sure he is aware of it. We'll tell Borin the next time he calls."

Katherine would have liked to do just that. She was fairly certain, however, that he did not intend to call again. But her uncle seemed so sure otherwise that she let herself hope. It had seemed as if the viscount enjoyed their company, even if he was not courting Constance or her. But the hours crawled by with no sign of him, and she had to own that her first reaction was correct. Lord Borin had had enough of the Collins family.

The knocker sounded at half past four, and she had to restrain herself from running to answer it. With an understanding smile, Bixby went to do his duty. Her spirits sank lower when a few minutes later he ushered in Lord Templeman.

Constance's cousin rolled into the withdrawing room in a none-too-clean brown coat and breeches and settled himself into one of the chairs with his customary creak. His pleased smile only served to sour Katherine's mood further.

"Miss Constance will be here shortly," Bixby said before leaving her alone with him. She could barely stand to look at his smug face, but she managed a tight smile for propriety's sake.

"And how are you today, Lord Templeman?"

"Excellent, Miss Collins. Are you enjoying your harp?"

She could honestly smile at that thought, and turned to gaze to at her instrument. "Yes, I am. I had not realized how much I missed it. Thank you for returning it to me."

"Well, don't just sit there," he said, folding flaccid hands over his bulging gut. "Play something. Let me see that my uncle's money wasn't wasted buying the thing for you."

Katherine gritted her teeth. "Unfortunately, the instrument requires additional tuning. You would not enjoy anything I played. Another time, perhaps."

Luckily, Constance entered then, saving her from further conversation. Templeman did not bother rising as the girl dropped a curtsy and sat across from him on the gilded settee.

"Welcome, Cousin," she murmured. "How good of you to visit."

"Duty," he replied. "It is my responsibility as head of this family to make sure you are cared for. Are you enjoying your Season?"

"Very much. We have attended any number of balls and fetes, met any number of interesting people."

"Gathered any number of suitors," Katherine put in maliciously.

Templeman cast her a glance of obvious annoyance before returning his gaze to Constance. "So I have heard. I also heard that despite my warnings, you persist in receiving Lord Borin."

Katherine opened her mouth to protest, but to her surprise, Constance spoke first.

"Lord Borin is a gentleman, Cousin. I am pleased to receive him whenever he deigns to call."

Katherine was not the only one surprised. Lord Templeman blinked at Constance's determined tone, then reddened.

"Then the more fool you. The man is a dastard. I would not be surprised if he turned out to be this spy who has everyone talking. He will be caught for espionage, you may be sure of it."

Constance gasped. Katherine sat straighter.

"Rumors like that," she informed him sternly, "can be very damaging, as I am certain you know, my lord."

"They can also serve as warnings to the innocent," Templeman countered.

"But surely you do not think Lord Borin in league with foreign agents," Constance protested. "He has been all that is gentlemanly and kind."

Templeman snorted, turning the vulgar sound into a cough behind his meaty hand. "Your loyalty does you credit, Cousin," he finally replied. "But enough of this. I had a purpose in coming today."

As if you didn't just achieve it, Katherine thought.

"And what would that be, Cousin?" Constance asked politely.

"Your birthday is in less than a month," he replied. "I thought perhaps I might throw you a party."

"Counting your money already?" Katherine accused.

"Katherine, really," Constance chided as Templeman bristled. "That is very considerate of you, Cousin. I would be delighted to have you host such a party."

"Good," he said, casting Katherine a triumphant

glance. "I have a number of friends I would like you to meet. If you have a few acquaintances you would like to invite as well, send me the list and I will see what can be done."

Constance agreed, and they chatted a few moments longer. Katherine could not bring herself to join the conversation. The man was insufferable, impossible. She was so appalled that after he took his leave, she rounded on her stepsister.

"Do you not see how selfish he is? He presumes to throw you a party but invites *his* friends."

"My cousin is simply focused on his own pursuits," Constance replied calmly. "I grant you he is somewhat lacking in the social arts . . ."

"Lacking?" Katherine burst out. "He tramples them at will! How can you stand to see your fortune go to him?"

She shrugged. "The money is not important to me. If it makes him happy, he is welcome to it."

"How can you say that! It is your father's money!"

"It is only money, Katherine." She eyed her sternly. "Keeping it in my possession will not bring Father back. Let it go."

Katherine wanted to go on fighting, but the look in Constance's eye was too determined. She sagged into her chair. "Then we are lost, Constance. I cannot help you if you will not help yourself."

"I am glad you finally realize that," she replied gently. "I cannot marry simply to keep my fortune, Katherine. If I do so, I make myself its servant."

Katherine nodded. "I understand. I do not like it, but I understand. You must do as your conscience bids you."

"Thank you," Constance murmured. "Now, I begin to believe you have calculated to the last penny how the loss of my fortune will affect us. What must we do if I do not find the perfect man in the next four weeks?"

Katherine could not resist one last try. "I found you the perfect man. You refused to pursue him."

"You found the perfect man for you. And you also refused to pursue him. Now, answer my question."

Katherine sighed. "We will lose the house and Bixby and Emma, too."

Constance bit her lip. "I suppose it could be worse. We might lose each other as well."

Katherine nodded. "Yes, there is that. Do not worry. I shall talk with Bixby and Emma tomorrow. Perhaps they might find a family who needs extra help for the Season."

"No, we won't," Bixby said from the doorway. Katherine and Constance turned to face him. "I won't leave you, Miss Katherine. Sir Richard and I have made do before and we will again. I'm sure Emma will feel the same way."

"But if . . . when Constance loses her fortune, we will not be able to pay you," Katherine explained, feeling tears starting. "We can't even afford this house."

"I don't need pay, miss, as long as I have family. Perhaps tomorrow I can send word to some friends. Surely we can find a nice house in the country where we can all be together."

"And we can have a garden," Constance said with a smile.

And we can grow into old maids together, Katherine thought, but she merely smiled and joined them in making plans. Time enough later to feel sorry for herself. It very much looked, in fact, as if she'd have the rest of her life.

But before she left London, there was one thing she had to do and that was to make sure Lord Borin was safe. If Sir Richard and Bixby wouldn't help her, she'd simply have to do it herself.

Alex's day was faring no better. He tried once again to return to his usual habits. He rose and spent an hour in fencing exercises before bathing and breakfasting. He joined his steward in reviewing his correspondence, then visited his solicitor to check on his financial affairs. Everything was disgustingly well run and efficient. No one needed him in the slightest.

He thought perhaps it might be different with his friends, but he had to own he had chosen a group of remarkably self-sufficient gentlemen with uncommon good sense. He was welcomed at any of their homes; they were pleased to have him join them in any of their pursuits. But no one was involved in anything particularly exciting or entertaining. Giles Sloan was on his way to listen to a niece practice for a violin solo. Sir Nigel Dillingham was being fitted for a new coat. Kevin Whattling was off to another prize fight. It was all very gentlemanly and downright boring.

Whatever way he looked at it, the zest was missing from his life. He wasn't sure when he'd lost it completely, but he was beginning to realize where it might be found. Even when the intrigue was past, he felt himself drawn to the Collins household.

Perhaps he should simply offer for his sprite. It very much looked as if he'd never get a chance to serve with Lord Hastings. He still could not claim to have learned why he was being followed. He had caught sight of his shadow twice during the day, but the creature was skittish enough that it disappeared if he so much as turned to look. He paid a likely lad to give chase at one point, but only ended up waiting on the street corner for an hour for the young fellow to return, and then with no more information than Alex had to begin with. At least his attempts seemed to scare the creature off for a bit.

But the sheer act of trying to catch his pursuers convinced him that offering for Miss Collins would be the wrong thing. He had to choose—a life of wife and responsibility or a life of daring and intrigue. Surely the latter was better suited to fill the void in his life. He would try again. The next time he was followed, he would not rest until the fellow was captured and questioned.

He had changed into his evening black and started for an early dinner at White's, as he often did, when he once more spotted the culprit. He was strolling along Old Bond Street, where most of the shops and offices were closing up from a long day. A few people hurried past in either direction, going home or to dinner like him. One more moving in his direction was hardly noticeable. But he spotted the fellow as soon as he fell into step.

He paused on the corner, trying to think as deviously as his opponent. Chasing obviously didn't work; he'd tried it too many times to his sorrow. The only one he'd ever caught was Eric Collins, and he knew now that his new opponents were much more cunning. So, perhaps he should let the fellow catch *him*.

He spotted a hack moving toward him and hailed it. The driver pulled over willingly.

"Where to, milord?"

Alex stepped closer to the box. "Don't turn your head until I finish talking, and then look as if you were checking to see whether you could turn the horses. There's a man following me. He's dressed in a long cloak, too dark and heavy for normal evening wear, and he keeps his head low. I'll give you a quid to wait a moment, then start for White's. If you come back this way in a quarter hour, I'll have another for you."

"I'm your man, milord," he promised.

"White's," Alex said, loudly enough for anyone to hear. He clambered into the coach, crossed the small interior and let himself out the other side. The driver waited as if making sure Alex was settled inside, then clucked to his horses and set off.

Alex dodged behind a passing coach and ducked into a shop door. Flattening himself against the wall in the deepening shadows, he waited. As he had expected, his pursuer hurried past a few moments later. This one must have been a youth. He looked much too short to be full grown, though Alex could see little of him in the voluminous hooded cape the fellow wore. His movements were also less confident, as if he were new to the role. Alex slipped in behind him with ease.

He followed him a short way, looking for an opportunity to corner the creature for a private conversation. His chance came moments later as they approached another narrow alley opening to the right. As his tormentor reached the space, Alex dashed forward and shoved him into the shadows.

Then he leaped in after him.

Seventeen

Katherine gasped as she was grabbed from behind. Before she could struggle, she was shoved into the alley and wrestled up against the wall so roughly that the hood from her cloak fell over her face. She'd been caught! Her assailant could only be the miscreant who had been following Lord Borin, who, unfortunately, was on his way to White's. If she was to escape, she had only herself to do it.

Heart hammering, she lashed out with her feet. Her leather half boots connected solidly with her assailant's leg. His grunt of pain was not nearly enough for the trouble he'd caused. But she did not have the strength to do greater damage. She took only a moment to be certain he was bent in agony before darting around him for the street.

"Oh, no, you don't!" He lunged after her, catching her about the knees. She fell hard onto the cobbles, knocking the breath from her. Rock gouged her hands through her gloves, but it was his voice that cut her most deeply. She rolled to stare up at the figure poised above her.

"Lord Borin?"

Ready to pounce, he froze. "Katherine?" He knelt, eyes wide, face paling, and pushed back the hood from her face. Her hair tumbled back with it, pins tinkling to the stones. "Dear God, it is you! Did I hurt you? Are you all right?"

His gaze about her person was frantic. She reached up an unsteady hand to touch his cheek, marveling at how sweet her name sounded from his lips.

"I'm quite all right, I assure you. It takes more than a bit of the rough and tumble to deter me."

He blew out a breath and pulled her close, hugging her to him. She felt his cheek against her hair. The wool of his coat warmed her skin. She could hear his heartbeat slowly returning to normal, while hers only seemed to speed at his nearness.

"Thank God," he murmured. "If I'd hurt you I would never have forgiven myself." He pulled back suddenly to eye her. "What on earth are you doing out this time of the evening? Do not tell me you are alone. Where is Sir Richard? Bixby?"

"Unavailable," she replied quickly before he could pepper more questions. "But we had seen you being followed last night. I could not stand by while you were in danger."

She hoped she did not sound as if she were maligning her uncle or Bixby's courage, or boasting of her own, but to her surprise, he stiffened, releasing her.

"And did it never occur to you that I might be able to take care of myself?"

She frowned. "Certainly. I simply did not know whether you were aware of the incident."

His fists clenched at his sides. "And you couldn't send me a note?"

She moved back from him, the anger in his voice confusing her. "Well, I suppose I could have, but how was I to know whether it would arrive in time or that your servants were not involved in the charade?"

"Oh, I see. Not only am I incapable of discovering

the miscreant on my tail and dealing with him, but I cannot even be trusted to pick reliable servants."

"That is not what I meant," she replied sternly, her own temper rising. "But if you persist in this nonsense you can save your own life next time."

"Not according to you." He glared at her a moment, then shook himself and sighed. "Forgive me. The thought that you would needlessly endanger your life for my sake drives me mad. I only wish you would trust me to take care of the situation." He took her elbow. "The hack should be returning shortly. Let me see you home."

She nodded, leaning against him as she climbed to her feet. His touch was firm, but cool. She had offended him.

She followed him to the street and stood silently as they waited for the hack. It hove into view moments later. Alex reached out and pulled her hood into place.

"Leave this to me," he ordered.

He was taking charge, as if she had no more sense than a pigeon on the steps of St. George's. She sighed. A managing woman would never be appreciated. She should have known better than to expect it from him.

The hack slowed at Alex's wave.

"Good work, milord," the coachman said, nodding to the huddled figure at Alex's side. "Do we take him to Bow Street?"

Alex shook his head, then opened the door and boosted Katherine inside. Turning to the hackman, he noticed that the man's eyes had widened.

"A ladybird?" he questioned. "I saw that petticoat as she mounted. Real nice catch, milord."

Alex threw him the promised gold piece. "Your passenger is a lady. I need not tell you that this conversation goes no further. We will take her home. Go to the mews behind Hyde Street. We'll walk from there."

The man pulled his forelock and turned to his horses. Alex climbed in and seated himself across from Katherine. The coach set off for Mayfair.

With the light from streetlamps coming through the windows, he could see that she sat primly, hands folded in her lap, face serene. If he hadn't known better, he would never have thought that she had just been caught in the middle of London alone in the dark.

"I begin to think you're actually proud of yourself," he accused, smiling in spite of himself.

She grinned back. "I was, rather." Then her grin faded. "Only I do not think you appreciated my help."

"I simply do not like the idea of you in danger," he repeated, but the set of her jaw told him she did not believe him. He supposed he had been a bit rude. Could she really not understand that her position was perilous? St. James was avoided by ladies after noon, being the province of gentlemen and their interests. She could have been accosted by a drunk, robbed by a footpad, kidnapped by a gang of youths out for fun at her expense. He felt chilled as he considered what might have happened to her at the hands of such ruffians.

"I hope you don't make a habit of this," he told her.

She refused to meet his gaze, staring instead out the window at the buildings. "What, managing people's lives, or wandering about the city in the dark?"

"The latter, assuredly, though I cannot imagine many people appreciate the former either." He knew he certainly didn't.

"They hate it," she replied coolly. "Unfortunately, they do not seem capable of managing their own lives without my help."

"And do you put me in that category?" he demanded, temper rising anew.

She sighed. "I confess that I did, once. But in coming to know you, I realize that you have a great deal of sense, for a man."

Despite himself, he chuckled. "Why do I get the feeling that is a far greater compliment than it appears?"

She turned to him with a smile. "Because you are intelligent as well. You are undoubtedly right that I should simply have sent you a note. But I suspect I wanted to be of service to you. Forgive me?"

He returned her smile. "There is nothing to forgive."

"Oh," she argued, smile fading, "but there is. I put you through all this trouble and I never spotted the real culprit who followed you."

He could feel her disappointment. She certainly had heart, this one. "I think he was scared off earlier in the day," he explained; then he cocked his head in interest. "What did you plan to do if you did spot him?"

She obviously had no concerns on the matter, for she shrugged. "Try to catch a glimpse of him and warn you. I know better than to accost someone bigger than me, my lord."

"But not a situation bigger than you," he guessed.

Her chin tipped up. "I never met a situation too big for me, until recently."

He knew her reference. "Your stepsister and her fortune."

She nodded, then sighed. "But that appears to have resolved itself."

"Has someone offered for her?" Alex asked with raised brow.

"No," she replied with another sigh. "She is resigned to losing her fortune. We agreed to start looking for homes outside London."

The thought of her leaving cut deep. "I am sorry to hear that."

"As am I. The one bright spot is that Bixby and Emma have agreed to come with us. We will be one happy family."

He frowned. "You sound anything but happy."

"I am selfish, I fear. Being together is what should matter. But, oh, how I shall miss London! The excitement, the bustle. The most intrigue we'll find in the country is guessing which of our neighbor's cows got into the cabbage last night."

He chuckled. "A rather dismal life, I quite agree. But take heart. You still have several weeks, and your stepsister's charms are considerable."

"She is a gem," she agreed readily. He was afraid she'd begin campaigning again and was relieved when she switched topics instead. "You will catch the villain who is following you, then?"

"Rest assured that I shall," he replied, although he wasn't entirely confident of his chances. He decided not to tell her that. He wanted no more of these episodes.

She leaned forward. "I have been terribly impertinent, my lord, having you followed, then doing so myself. Would you stand one more question, as very likely we shall not see each other again?"

His heartbeat quickened as his gaze met hers. "Ask anything you like."

She hesitated a moment, and he leaned forward expectantly. He could see her swallow. "You aren't connected with the foreign agents, are you?" she asked carefully.

He flinched, then barked out a laugh. "That was not

what I expected you to ask, but no. I assure you, I would never connect myself with the enemy."

She nodded sagely. "I knew it. I simply wanted to hear it from your own lips." She paused as he leaned back, then asked quietly, "What did you think I was going to ask?"

He smiled ruefully. "To tell you would make me the greatest coxcomb."

"I have certainly played the arrogant fool for you," she replied with a smile. "I can hardly complain if you choose to do likewise."

He watched her. Lamplight glowed on the auburn curls escaping her hood and lit her eyes with cool fire. Could he be so bold? She said they might never see each other again. He knew she was right. Unless he moved himself, she would slip out of his life far more quietly than she had entered.

"I thought, Miss Collins," he said, "that you might ask me to kiss you again."

Her eyes widened. She licked her lips as if imagining the feel of his. That was all it took to heave his willing body across the coach and pull her into his embrace.

Her kiss was full of sweet promise, her body as willing as his to touch, to hold, to caress. He felt his heartbeat speed, his breath quicken. This was the excitement he craved, this closeness the herb required to spice his predictable life. He knew in that instant that he would do anything to keep her with him, his sprite, his Katherine, his love.

He broke off the kiss, hugging her close, struggling with the emotions that surged through him. Love? Yes, it was love. He could feel it filling the empty spaces inside him. He wanted to protect her, to cherish her. He didn't want her miles away in some country retreat. He didn't want to spend years in a foreign country behind enemy lines. He wanted the daily excitement of growing old with her. The very idea stunned him, and he could only sit and lean his chin against her temple in wonder.

She must have noticed his sudden quiet, for she pulled back to look into his face. "What is it?"

He was amazed his love wasn't glowing from every inch of his face. He also found himself at a loss to explain the transformation to her. She had made no secret of the fact that she admired him. She certainly seemed to enjoy his kisses as much as he enjoyed kissing her. But did she love him in return?

"Lord Borin?" she pressed, moving out of his arms. "What is it? Did I do something wrong?"

He found himself laughing, and she recoiled further. He reached out and pulled her back into his arms. "No, no, Katherine, you mistake me. You have done nothing wrong. On the contrary, I would say you have done everything right."

He could feel her frown. "I don't understand."

"Neither do I, I assure you." He chuckled again. "Miss Collins, Katherine, would you do me the honor of allowing me to speak to your guardian?"

"Why?" She pulled away again, and he merely smiled at her. He rather thought it was a besotted sort of smile. He hadn't felt this light-headed since drinking his first bottle of Madeira. Her eyes widened as if she understood at last.

"I . . . I would be only too delighted to have you speak to Sir Richard," she stammered. "But my lord, Alexander, are you certain?"

"Faith, my girl, I am not certain about anything at the moment," he assured her. "Except the fact that the idea of you leaving London, going anywhere, doing anything, without me by your side makes me physically ill."

Her lower lip quivered, and he moved himself to taste it again. She threw her arms about his neck and gave herself over to their embrace. This time he let his emotions sweep them both away.

A discrete cough warned him something was wrong. Raising his head, he realized the coach had been stopped for some time and the driver was standing at the side, waiting for Alex to notice his presence.

He reluctantly released Katherine. Her lips were swollen from his kisses, her hair wild from his caress, her eyes dreamy. He imagined he looked no less seduced. He raked a hand back through his hair and pulled up her hood.

"We're a few doors down from the house," he murmured in explanation. "Let me send off the driver, and I'll walk you the rest of the way."

She nodded, and he proceeded to do just as he had said. He marveled that some part of him could still think. It was difficult to walk beside her to the back garden of the Collins house, but allowing her to leave his side was the hardest thing he had done. He consoled himself with the fact that he would not have to wait much longer before she could stay with him forever. He watched until she was safely in the kitchen door, then turned to go.

If anyone followed him home, he was feeling entirely too well-to-live to notice.

Eighteen

Katherine nearly floated into the house. She was so enchanted, in fact, that she was halfway across the kitchen before realizing that Emma and Bixby were sitting at the worktable staring at her. She paused and returned their gazes. The expectant looks on their faces told her they had been waiting for her. Unfortunately, she couldn't seem to remember why.

Bixby rose. "I knew as soon as Miss Constance came looking for you that you had gone after his lordship. I fobbed her off. Well, Miss Katherine? Did you catch the fellow?"

She gave him a lopsided smile before realizing he wasn't talking about Alex. "Oh, the spy. No, I didn't. But Lord Borin is aware of the danger and will take steps to rectify matters."

Emma threw up her hands as she too rose. "Oh, Miss Katherine, how could ye go out by yerself like that! What were ye thinking, child?"

At the moment, she wasn't thinking at all. She was feeling her blood sing, her spirit soar. "I'm just fine, Emma," she assured her housekeeper.

"Of course she is," Bixby said, pride evident in his voice as he came around the table. "She was doing her duty, putting her conscience before propriety. If you ask me, that's the mark of a true lady."

Conscience before propriety? She rather thought it was her emotions, not her conscience, that had the upper hand. But she really didn't want to discuss that with Bixby. "Yes, well," she hedged, edging for the door to the upper floors, "I think I shall just turn in."

"Oh, come on, miss," Bixby begged, holding out a chair for her. "Sit down and tell an old campaigner all about it. Did you at least spot the miscreant? What did he look like? Does Lord Borin think him connected with the spy or Miss Montgomery?"

Katherine shook her head. Her emotions were far too thick to sit and have a nice coze. She saw Emma regarding her with a frown and felt her smile slipping.

"Enough of you, Willy Bixby," the housekeeper said suddenly. "Can ye not see the poor girl's done in?" She ambled forward and put a thick arm about Katherine's waist. "There, my dear, ye just go on up to yer room. I'll bring water for a nice hot bath. 'Twill do ye a world of good."

Bixby's face fell, but he made no move to stop her as she gave Emma a grateful hug and fled.

She tried not to think about the scene in the coach while she changed out of her clothes. If she continued to dwell on it she would get nothing done the rest of her life! But once she immersed herself in the steamy water of the bathing tub she found she had shed her control with her clothes. Memories and emotions tumbled over each other and she knew her tears contributed to the water around her.

And why should she cry? He loved her! That could be the only explanation for his words and actions. Nothing on the walls of her War Office had indicated he trifled with ladies of the *ton*. While she was certainly not in his social sphere, neither was she the sort to be made a mistress. And had he been willing to overlook that fact, he could have taken the first move tonight. She did not think she would have been able to stop him had he demanded more from her than sweet kisses and a passionate embrace. She had been enjoying herself far too much.

But he had made no move to dishonor her. Instead, he said he wished to call on Sir Richard. The only reason would be to offer for her. Why did she find that so hard to believe?

Perhaps because she heard so many complaints about her skills and abilities. Oh, she knew her family loved her, but at times she felt as if a spot deep inside her was empty. No one but her family had ever truly listened to her play the harp, until Alex. No one but her stepfather had ever praised her ability to manage a household or keep their family intact, except Alex. Few had ever noted that she was pretty in her own right, that she might have as much charm in her own way as the lovely Constance, but Alex did. That someone as handsome and kind and charming as Alex could actually love someone like her was beyond her wildest dreams. She wanted it to be true. *Oh, please, God, let it be true!* She could imagine nothing finer than to be the wife of Alexander Wescott, Viscount Borin. She hiccuped, half sob, half laugh. The hope he had offered her was too amazing to believe, and too wonderful to let go.

Katherine must have been more tired from her exertions than she had thought, for she slept far later than was her wont the following morning. She found the breakfast table deserted and only curdling chocolate left for her to drink. Curious, she went to the withdrawing room, where she found Constance reading a book.

"Where is everyone?" she asked.

"Good morning, sleepyhead," her stepsister greeted with a smile. Her pink lustring gown was fresh, her curls glossy. Even though she had bathed the night before, Katherine felt dusty in her gray poplin.

"Eric is supposed to be at his studies with Sir Richard," her stepsister continued, "and Bixby went to answer the door."

Katherine stiffened. "The door? A bit early for callers, is it not?"

Constance pushed out her lower lip thoughtfully. "I suppose so. It must have been a tradesman to keep him so long."

"At the front door?" Katherine shook her head as her heart started to beat faster. "Not likely." Turning to go, Katherine saw Constance set down her book and rise.

"What is it?" she called after her with obvious concern. "Has something happened?"

Katherine paused in the doorway. "I don't know," she admitted, "but I intend to find out."

She knew her stepsister was at her heels as she hurried to the stair and down it. She saw no one until she reached the ground floor. The door was shut, the entryway empty. Peering around the stair, however, she found Bixby and Eric in deep study at the library door. Bixby leaned with one ear to the oak panel while Eric knelt with one eye squinting in the keyhole.

"What on earth are you doing?" Katherine demanded.

Bixby's head jerked up. "Shh!" he cautioned, waving her to his side. "Lord Borin is in there with Sir Richard."

"What?" Katherine flew down the corridor. She

joined Bixby with her ear to the door, but only succeeded in hearing muffled voices.

"How long have they been in there?" she whispered to the butler as Constance tiptoed down the corridor, eyes wide.

"A few minutes," the butler murmured. "You should have seen his face at the door, miss. I never saw a man so tense. Was he angry you followed him last night?"

Katherine frowned. He had come angry? Had she totally misunderstood him? He had called speaking to Sir Richard an honor. Surely that meant an offer of marriage.

"You followed Lord Borin last night?" Eric asked. "Oh, would I have given a quid to see that!"

"Katherine, you didn't," Constance chided.

Before she could answer, Bixby hushed them all again. "Quiet! Do you want to get us caught before we learn why Lord Borin came?"

"He's no doubt here to offer," Constance said sagely, crossing her arms over her chest. "It is his duty to protect Katherine's reputation."

Duty? Her heart plummeted. With all her stratagems, had she managed only to compromise herself and him in the process? She had no doubt he desired her, but she didn't want him if all he felt was lust and duty.

Bixby had returned his ear to the door.

"What's happening?" Constance begged in a whisper. "What are they saying?"

"Shh!" Katherine said in unison with Bixby. She didn't know whether she could stand to find out, but found she certainly couldn't stand to wait wringing her hands like Constance. She pasted her ear to the door once more.

They were so intent in their studies that no one heard

the rap on the front door or its repetition several seconds later.

Lord Templeman frowned when no one came to answer his knock. He glanced to where his carriage waited beside that bearing the Borin crest. His spies had come to warn him the minute they'd spotted the viscount. The wretch had broken his word and come calling yet again. It remained to be seen how far matters had gotten. He had come immediately to find out.

But he couldn't find out anything if they didn't answer the blasted door. He glanced about again, noticing that none of the neighbors was in evidence. He shifted his bulk to hide his movements from the coachmen and grooms, then pressed on the door handle. To his delight, it opened easily and silently. He peered into the entry.

He was not prepared, however, for the sight that met his eyes. His cousin stood beside the library door, wringing her hands. Their miserable excuse for a butler had the effrontery to lean against the door, listening. If Templeman wasn't very much mistaken, that was the brazen Miss Collins partially hidden behind her butler doing the exact same thing. He even spotted her brother at the keyhole. A nastier group of petty spies he'd never seen. He puffed up his chest to reveal them, loudly, but before he could open his mouth, Bixby stiffened.

"There! Did you hear that, Miss Katherine? He offered!"

Constance cried out and threw her arms about her stepsister while the boy jumped from the door and began doing a hornpipe in the corridor. Bixby grinned from ear to ear.

Templeman stumbled back out the door and closed

it silently behind him. Clutching his heart, he managed to reach the coach, waving his man to drive on.

Collapsing against the velvet cushions, he gulped in air. This was so much worse than he had feared. Offered! Borin had offered for Constance. There was no question that Sir Richard would accept, or that his cousin would have any regrets in agreeing. Borin was titled, Borin was well connected, Borin was disgustingly, impossibly rich. With so much wealth, why would he insist on separating Templeman from his own rightful fortune? Had he not done everything from the start to dissuade Constance from this union? Yet, despite his best efforts at rumormongering and innuendo, Borin had not been shunned.

Well, the time for subtlety had passed. Borin must disappear, as soon as possible. And he knew just the way to do it. He rapped on the panel over his head.

His coachman answered with alacrity. "Yes, milord?"

"Take me to Whitehall," he growled. "I'm long past due for an appointment with the War Office."

Inside the library, Alex paced the floor, intent on making his case to a surprisingly stern judge.

"I know I have not shown myself overly industrious in catching this spy," he said to Sir Richard, who had been watching him with a light in his eyes that Alex found unnerving. "But I assure you I will be a devoted husband to your niece."

"And do you intend to continue your quest to serve in the War Office?" Sir Richard asked with maddening calm.

"I do not," Alex promised.

Sir Richard raised a brow. "Do you give up so easily, then?"

Alex could not help but wince. Here was his failing, come back to haunt him. He had to show the man that he could be counted upon to take care of Katherine. "I have been told that I do not have it in me to work for what I want," he confessed. "But I will work for your niece's hand, if that is what you require. Name a task, and it shall be done. Test me and I will succeed."

"Commendable," Sir Richard replied with a quirk of his lips that told Alex he was trying hard not to laugh at him. Instead of taking umbrage, he could only smile in return.

"Then you'll set me some task to prove my worth?"

"Not so fast," the man replied, raising his hand as if to forestall additional questions. "I have some questions for you and an issue you must resolve. First, if not the hard work, why have you decided against a career with the War Office?"

Alex saw no reason not to be forthcoming. "I had thought it was excitement I craved, but I have found all I could hope for in your niece. I love Katherine, Sir Richard, and I would be honored to spend the rest of my life with her."

"I rather think she feels the same way about you," he replied, and Alex felt his heart jump at the prospect. "I think you have a great deal to offer Katherine— reputation, place in society, wealth. Unfortunately, at the moment, you also offer her a shadow of suspicion. That is the issue you must address."

Alex grimaced. "This damnable spying affair."

Sir Richard nodded. "You appear to be no closer to solving the mystery of your pursuers than when we first met. I assume it has something to do with your connection to Lord Hastings."

"Possibly," Alex replied. "At the moment, however, I wish I had never laid eyes on the chap. I want this to end."

"I believe you, my boy. But someone doesn't. And until we know who, I cannot be comfortable with your engagement to my niece."

Alex felt his shoulders sag. "You are right, of course. Yet I fear the damage to her reputation by her recent escapades. And, selfishly, I do not wish to wait to call her my own. Can you not trust me to extricate myself from this matter honorably?"

Sir Richard eyed him, and Alex held his breath. When he thought surely he had lost, the man struck his hands on the arms of the leather-upholstered chair.

"Very well," he proclaimed. "We will leave it to Katherine. If she'll have you, you have my blessing."

Alex blew out a breath, springing forward to pump the man's hand as he rose. "Thank you, Sir Richard. I promise you I will make her happy."

"Of that, I have no doubt," Sir Richard replied with a smile. "Go on, now. Have Bixby fetch her for you. I will leave you two alone. If things go as you plan, I hope you will stay to lunch to celebrate."

Alex readily agreed, accompanying Sir Richard to the door. He thought he heard a wild shuffling as they approached, but it could have been the pounding of his pulse.

Bixby was in place at the foot of the stairs as Sir Richard opened the door and, to Alex's delight, Katherine was with him. He noted that she looked unreasonably pale, but he was too pleased to see her to wonder at the reason. Sir Richard gave him an encouraging wink before crossing to his niece.

"How fortunate to find you here, Katherine. Lord Borin has something he wishes to say to you. I've given him permission to meet you in the library." He gave her shoulder a squeeze.

As she moved forward, Alex couldn't help noticing her reticence. She walked as if she were going to her execution. His heart plummeted once more. Had he misunderstood her last night? Did she not wish him to offer? It couldn't be that she was afraid of the spy after all, not his courageous Katherine. Bemused, he bowed her before him into the library and shut the door behind them.

"Before you start," she said, head high, "you need to know that I refuse. I will not marry you."

Nineteen

Katherine watched as Alex paled. She waited for a sign of the relief she knew he must feel at her announcement. Instead of thanking her for relieving him of his duty, however, he stayed by the door, holding himself still.

"I apologize, of course," he said slowly, "if I have offended you by my offer. But I thought you understood my intentions last night."

"As did I," she assured him. She was about to say more, but she heard a faint thump from the door. He must have heard it, too for he turned and eyed the panel with a curious frown. She did not have to wonder at the noise. This was one conversation she intended to keep private. "Excuse me a moment," she told him.

He moved out of her way as she approached the door. She yanked it open. Eric tumbled to the floor, and Bixby had to grab Constance's arm to prevent her from doing likewise. Katherine put her hands on her hips.

"Upstairs," she ordered, "all of you. Now. I will tell you what you need to know later."

Eric scrambled to his feet, face as red as her stepsister's. Bixby was more sanguine.

"Come on, you lot," he urged. "Best thing to do when you're caught is beat a hasty retreat."

"I thought it was to bluff it out," Eric protested.

"Bit late for that," Alex advised him with a smile. Eric grimaced.

"We do beg your pardon, my lord," Constance said prettily as Bixby shooed them toward the stairs. Katherine leaned out the door to watch them climb. She started to shut the door, then spied another head peering from the dining room.

"Uncle," she warned. With a sheepish grin, he ducked back out of sight.

She snapped shut the library door with a frustrated sigh.

"An enterprising group," Alex quipped as she turned to face him.

"Most assuredly," she replied. "Now, where were we?"

He closed the distance between them. "I believe we were right about here." His arms slipped around her as his mouth claimed hers.

Oh, she should protest, push him away. She wanted no marriage not based on love. But the touch of his lips was so sweet, so delicious, she could not seem to stop herself from taking more. She let herself glory in the feel of him one last time, how his mouth moved against hers, how his hands caressed her back, how his strong body made her feel protected, cherished. She let the kiss go on as long as he liked. It would be over all too soon, she feared.

At last he raised his head. Passion danced in his eyes and with it, determination. "Miss Collins," he murmured, "will you not reconsider my offer?"

He could not know how tempted she was to do just that. Why not simply give in and spend her life with this wonderful man? Yet would it be a life? Lust, however hot, must cool eventually. Without love, what else was there on which to build a strong union? She would stand for nothing less.

"I cannot, in good conscience," she replied, moving purposely out of his arms. "I thank you for wanting to protect my reputation, my lord, but I cannot marry you simply as a duty."

He frowned. "Duty? Is that what you feel when you kiss me?"

She felt herself color. "No, certainly not! But excellent kisses a marriage do not make."

"I quite agree. A marriage should be based on mutual compatibility, likeness of mind, commonality of goals."

"Not love?" There, she'd said it, even if it was only in a rather pathetic little squeak.

He pulled her back against him. "Of course love. Oh, I grant you any number of *ton* marriages lack that. I will also grant you I was rather naive in that area. Until I met you."

Katherine gazed up at him. His smile was tender, and his eyes glowed with an emotion she was afraid to name. "Oh, Alex, if only I could believe you."

He stroked the hair at her temple. "Why can't you believe me, my heart? I tell you I love you, and I wish to marry you. Why is that so impossible to believe?"

"We have not known each other long," Katherine demurred. She caught herself toying with the gold filigree button on his waistcoat and forced her hand down. What was this? She wasn't some dewy-eyed debutante. She forced herself to look up at him, to name the fear that held her. "You don't really know me."

His smile deepened. "Don't I? You are intelligent, courageous, and true. Who wouldn't love you?"

Her heart constricted. "A great many people. You name only my positive traits, my lord."

"They say love is blind," he teased. "I find myself so besotted that I cannot see the many faults you no doubt think you have."

That was exactly what she feared. Her throat was so tight she wondered that she could still speak. "Then allow me to list them for you. I am an arrogant, head-strong, managing female."

He shrugged. "I have been known to be arrogant and headstrong myself. Look at this situation with the spy."

"Yes, look at that," she urged. "I believe you can love me because you think I will bring excitement to your life. Day-to-day living is far less romantic, I fear. You would tire of me far too quickly."

"Nonsense," he averred. "I have dealt with that is-sue. It isn't espionage I seek, Katherine, it's you."

"It cannot be." She pulled away again. Each time it grew more difficult. "Do you honestly say that you could love a managing woman?"

"Certainly. So long as she did not attempt to manage me."

Katherine closed her eyes in desperation. "But I did, Alex. And I fear I would do it again. I cannot seem to stop myself."

"You tried to interest me in your stepsister. How is that so very bad?"

If only he knew. "You must believe me," she replied. "You may be followed by spies, but I have my own demons to keep me company. I would never suit you, Alex."

"I won't believe that," he declared. "Your uncle threatened to make me deal with my pursuers first be-fore requesting your hand, and I refused because I could not stand the notion of waiting to hear you ac-cept. Don't hold me off, Katherine. I love you."

"Do you?" Fury rose from deep inside her. "Do

you really? Very well, my lord. I will give you an opportunity to prove it. Come with me."

She seized his hand and tugged him to the door, throwing it open once more. Sir Richard barely managed to get out of her way in time. His face was red as he scrambled into the entry.

"Is nothing sacred in this house?" Alex asked as Katherine ignored her floundering uncle and plowed for the stairs.

"Absolutely nothing," Katherine clipped.

He did not resist her as she led him up to the attic. She did not dare look at his face. He thought she was so wonderful; he saw only what she had let him see. Time enough that he saw her as she really was. She marched up to the door of her War Office and threw it open.

"There!" she proclaimed, dropping his hand to gesture at the walls. "There is the real Katherine Collins, a woman so coldhearted that she could determine her prey and not rest until she had captured it. Look at this and tell me you love me!"

Alex stared at the walls. At first all he saw were pieces of paper tacked to plaster. She had opened the door so quickly that they still fluttered with the breeze, like so many birds attempting to take wing. He had no idea what she was trying to show him, but she was so determined that he had no choice but to wander closer. As he did so, his life materialized in minute detail.

He moved from note to note as his emotions moved from surprise to admiration to annoyance. She knew when he rose, what he ate for breakfast, when he left the house, what he did, with whom he did it, and when he returned home. She knew he had a secret passion for sweetmeats and found the color purple erotic. She had the name of his valet, his tailor, his friends, and his mistress. The last brought him up short, but the note below it made him suck in a breath.

" 'Sent ruby to Miss Montgomery'?" he read. Turning, he stared at Katherine. "You had the temerity to turn out my mistress?"

She shrugged, but the color in her cheeks belied her calm. "It was necessary. You would never have made an offer if she were still available to you."

Comprehension dawned and with it revulsion so strong it burned his gut. "You planned this. You played on my emotions to elicit an offer of marriage."

"Guilty," she said, making his fists ball at her breezy reply.

He could not seem to grasp the enormity of the offense. Glancing from one piece of paper to another, he shook his head. "Was your stepsister's fortune a humdrum? Was Lord Templeman's bravura part of the game? By God, it was a neat trap."

"And you nearly fell into it," she replied. "You see why I say you cannot love me, my lord?"

Blood roared in his ears. "Love you? Madam, I never even knew you. The woman I fell in love with was a fiction."

Her smile was tight. "Then you won't mind taking yourself off?"

"Nothing could induce me to stay." He brushed past her, the brief touch raising bile in his throat. He stormed down the stairs, snatched his hat off the hall table, and slammed the door behind him.

"Home," he barked to his startled coachman. He leaped up into the carriage and threw the lap robes out of the way. To think he had been so anxious to make his case this morning that he had rung for his carriage rather than walk.

For what? To be made a fool, to have his heart

ripped from his chest and trampled upon with wild glee. He wanted to throttle her. He wanted to pretend he'd never met her. He wanted to erase the memory of her face from his mind and her touch from his body. Hastings was right—he would never have made an agent. He was entirely too dim-witted, hot tempered, and puffed up with his own consequence. Small wonder the man had refused him. Small wonder Katherine had refused him.

The sweet light of logic pierced his dark thoughts. Why had she refused him? She had had him, heart in hand, ready to lay it at her feet at but a word from her. After all that work, why refuse?

He took a deep breath and forced his emotions to calm. Something wasn't right. Was he still being manipulated? Why had she balked with the prize in hand? She had schemed and planned to trap him. Could it be that her courage had failed in the end?

No, not her courage. He had called her courageous, and even this revelation could not change that image. Miss Collins hadn't a cowardly bone in her body. Even if she wasn't the woman he thought, her actions spoke for themselves in that regard. She had trailed spies and confronted men twice her size. So if it wasn't fear that motivated her, then what?

Could it be that her conscience had pricked her? If she were as wicked as he'd painted her, it seemed odd for her to suddenly realize her guilt. Perhaps she was worried how he would react if he learned the truth, but if she'd simply agreed to his proposal he would have been honor bound to wed her, deceitful chit or not. She had hooked one of the biggest trout in the stream and deliberately set it free. Was all this some demented game?

No, that he could not believe. The affection, the genuine love he'd felt among the Collins family could not have been faked. Sir Richard's passion for his country could not be false. Eric and Miss Templeman truly cared for each other and the rest of their family. Katherine's passion for her music was equally fervent, as was her ceaseless devotion to her stepsister, brother, and uncle. A woman who loved and lived like that could not be a scheming temptress.

What then? Had she truly schemed only to find a husband for Miss Templeman? Her ways were unconventional, but her purpose was sound. Her activities were not much different from what he hoped to accomplish with Lord Hastings. And if Templeman's greed was no fabrication, she had greater need. Was the real Katherine so different from the woman he had imagined?

He shook his head. He'd been a fool. Instead of railing at her, he should have delved more deeply into what she was trying to say. She had let him believe her a schemer when in truth she was simply far more skilled at management than he could ever be. And she didn't think that trait very lovable. That was what she meant by the demons that hounded her—she doubted her worth. He was not fool enough to think his love would be the one thing to turn that tide, but at least he could tell her how wrong she was. Her ability to plan and carry out her campaign was exactly the trait so often missing in himself. She was clever, courageous, and spirited, exactly the kind of person he wished to become. She wasn't afraid to work, if through that work she could help the people she loved. Together, they might make the perfect marriage.

He almost had his man turn the carriage around, but somehow he didn't think she was ready to hear words of love from him just yet. The pain would be too fresh. He would give her a day to calm and then renew his suit.

Miss Templeman might be a gem, but Katherine Collins was a diamond of the first water and he refused to let her slip through his fingers because of his misplaced pride and her stubborn heart.

He was actually feeling rather hopeful when he entered his town house. The hope changed to something else when he learned that Davis Laughton was waiting for him. Handing his hat to his butler, he hurried to the library.

Laughton had been sitting in one of the chairs, but he rose as Alex entered. With his brown hair and eyes and slender build, Laughton looked more like an Oxford scholar than the cream of Lord Hastings's staff, as Alex knew him to be. His gaze this morning was cool, and Alex felt his gut clench anew.

"Good afternoon, Lord Borin," he said politely. "Lord Hastings would like a moment of your time. I have been asked to escort you to the War Office. Immediately."

Twenty

Katherine came down the stairs more slowly in Alex's wake. It was done. She had been noble and let him see her true self. She was not surprised that he had rejected her. She was only surprised it hurt so much.

Constance and Eric were peering out the withdrawing room door. It was a guess as to whose eyes were wider.

"You showed him the War Office," Eric guessed.

"The what?" Constance asked.

"The War Office," Katherine told her, amazed she could be so calm. "It is across from the schoolroom. We studied Lord Borin quite thoroughly before presenting him to you. We had his entire life neatly cataloged on the walls. We listed his likes, dislikes, strengths, and weaknesses. And now he knows ours. I thought it was only fair."

Eric grimaced. "Was he awfully mad?"

"Tremendously," Katherine replied, trying not to remember the hurt and anger on his face. "We shall not hear from him again unless it is through his solicitor calling us before the magistrates."

Eric paled as Constance gasped. "The magistrates? Surely you did nothing criminal."

"Perhaps not," Katherine allowed, "although I would think there might be some prohibition against trapping a man into marriage for material gain."

"But that's not what you did," Constance protested. "He wanted to marry you. You wanted to marry him. You love him."

"That is immaterial," Katherine snapped. "I am a managing female. Lord Borin should be thankful to be rid of me."

"You are a skilled administrator," Sir Richard corrected, coming up the stairs. "And Borin would be lucky to have you beside him, as would any fellow."

Katherine raised her head, hoping he would not see the pain that must be blazing from her eyes. "A shame he did not see fit to agree with you, Uncle."

"A greater shame that you do not agree with me, Katherine," he chided.

"Agree with you?" She felt tears coming and dashed them away. Could none of them understand? "How can I agree with you? I have too much evidence to the contrary."

"Who would say such a thing to you?" Constance cried.

"You!" When they stared at her, Katherine rushed on. "Eric complains endlessly that I manage him. Constance encourages me to pursue more womanly activities, as if managing this house is somehow unmaidenly. And Sir Richard tells me he must take over my responsibilities, as if somehow it is wrong of me to do them when I am far better at them than he is."

Her voice had risen with each sentence. She sounded a veritable shrew! She pressed her lips together to hold back the frustration, but she knew her eyes were daring them to disagree with her. Her uncle regarded her sadly, and Constance stared at her with tears in her own eyes. She couldn't stand their pity. For the first time in her life, she fled.

She was thankful they did not immediately follow her to the room she shared with Constance, leaving her to sob her eyes out alone. She should not have lost her temper with them. They only spoke the truth. This drive she felt to line things up nicely and neatly was a curse. She could not fix the world's problems—she could not fix their problems. She couldn't even fix her own.

But crying had never helped much. The tears let out her anger, but they could not relieve the weight on her heart. Even in trying to get Alex to see her as she was, she had lied. She let him think she sought him for herself. It wasn't so very different from the truth, she supposed. She had not trusted him to make the decision she wanted, and so she had set out to manage him to her wishes. She could not help it that her wishes had changed along the way.

It was not long before her natural inclination to order reasserted itself. She sat up from where she lay crying and wiped the tears off her cheeks. She had work to do. Like it or not, her management skills would be needed if they were to remove themselves from London for the country. She had a house to find, furniture to sell or give away, clothes and belongings to pack. It was going to take a great deal of work to leave town. It might even be enough to help her forget Alex.

But she doubted that.

She had washed her face and tidied her hair by the time there was a tap at her door. When she called admittance, Eric poked his head in.

"Are you ready for company?"

She smiled. "Certainly. What do you need?"

He made a face, wandering into the room. "Must I need something? Can't I just wish to be with you?"

"Certainly," she repeated. She waited for him to come farther into the room, but he stopped at the end of her bed, shifting uneasily from foot to foot. With a smile, she moved to his side and hugged him. With a pang, she noted that his head came just under her chin, when it had been at her breastbone only months before. He was growing up. What a shame they would never be able to send him to Eton or Oxford or give him any of the other advantages their father and stepfather would have wanted.

As Eric pulled away from her, his face was screwed up in obvious guilt.

"All right," she said, putting hands on her hips. "Out with it. What have you come to confess?"

"Nothing!" he protested, head shaking vehemently. When she continued to regard him, he shrugged. "Oh, all right. I lied. I do need you. We need you. There's something you must see in the War Office."

Katherine shook her head. "I have no desire to go there ever again. You may tell Bixby to pull down the pins and burn the notes."

"May I help?" he asked eagerly.

"Of course. But help only. We hardly need bonfires in the attic."

She thought that would end the matter, but he took her hand and gave it a tug. "Please, Katherine, come with me. I promised I'd bring you, and a gentleman does not go back on his word."

His determination only reminded her of Alex. She resisted his pull. "What is this about?"

He only tugged harder, managing to make her feet slide on the carpet. "Just come and you'll see."

She wanted to continue resisting, but she somehow doubted he would relent. He was too much like her in that regard. Reluctantly, she let him lead her back to the scene of her defeat. Constance, Sir Richard, Emma, and Bixby were waiting for her just inside the door to the War Office.

"What is this?" Katherine demanded.

Sir Richard snapped a salute with a grimace at the pain it obviously caused his leg. "Simply continuing our duty, Colonel. As you can see, we have another person under surveillance now."

She frowned, peering into the room. The arrangement of the papers had been changed. Moving closer, she saw that they were fresh sheets, hastily scrawled, the ink still dripping in places. She spotted Constance's elegant scroll, her uncle's scrawl, and Eric's painstakingly correct lettering. She could not tell what they intended.

"Who?" she asked. "Why?"

"I shall take the last question," Sir Richard replied, "and let the others take the first. The person in question is acting against her best interests and, as caring individuals, we must intervene."

Her brow cleared. "I have given up interfering with Constance's life. This is not necessary."

"I disagree," Constance put in with a smile. "I am not the person in question. This person is far more essential to the well-being of this family."

"Or at least just as essential," Sir Richard amended. "She keeps me from making a fool of myself on a regular basis."

Katherine offered him a small smile and started to protest, but the others were obviously not about to let her get a word in.

"She encourages me to take on responsibilities," her brother added proudly, "so that I may grow up to be a respected gentleman. That is a very good thing, even if I do grouse about it from time to time."

Katherine reached out to ruffle his hair. He ducked under her hand with a grin.

"She be none too proud to take up a kettle or sewing needle to help her family," Emma put in with a proud smile. "She does what's needed to see they be cared for, regardless of her own wishes."

Katherine found it harder to smile, even though her heart wished to do so.

Bixby had no such difficulties. "And she's not above a bit of danger," he added with a grin. "Particularly for the sake of others. She didn't balk at chasing a spy about in the dark. Nor did she balk at serving beside an old man who should have been put out to pasture long ago. She gave him a purpose, a bit of excitement to liven up his retirement."

"And she helped a blind man see," Sir Richard said, stepping up to take her hand as she felt her tears start anew. "And a lame man realize he had more to give his country, and his family, than a pair of legs."

"You make me sound a saint," Katherine said with a sniff. "I assure you I am not."

"Neither are you such a dark sinner," her uncle protested. "Your gift is administration, my dear. You may not always use it to its best advantage, but your heart is in the right place."

She could not seem to let the matter go so easily. "But I interfere with your lives."

"We understand that you do it because you care about us," Constance answered her. "We are quite capable of telling you when you go too far."

"Yes," Katherine said, remembering, "you do that rather well."

"There you have it, then," Sir Richard maintained. "Don't see your ability as an evil, Katherine. In fact, if I remember my schooling, the Bible says it is no less than a gift from God."

Katherine stared at him. "Truly?"

"Truly. Perhaps I can find you the reference."

"First Corinthians twelve: twenty-eight," Constance supplied helpfully.

From off in the distance came the sound of the door knocker.

"Duty," Bixby said. He squeezed her shoulder as he hurried from the room.

Constance, Emma, and Eric encircled her.

"We just wanted you to know how we feel, Miss Katherine," their housekeeper murmured, eyes bright. "Any man would be lucky to have ye, and that's a fact."

"And we are lucky to have you," Constance assured her, giving her a hug.

Katherine laughed through her tears. "And I am lucky to have all of you. Thank you for reminding me of that."

Sir Richard patted her shoulder. "Then let's have no more of these tears. Let us put our energies into discussing this matter with Lord Borin."

Katherine's smile faded as they pulled away. "It is impossible. I closed that door."

"And he slammed it," Eric muttered.

"Then let us open a window," Constance insisted. "There must be some way to reach him."

"We know enough about him," Eric mused. "We must have something we can use."

"Not again," Katherine said. "I'm learning that there are places to apply this so-called gift and places to leave it aside. I will not use any information we gathered about Lord Borin to appeal to him."

"Simply telling him you love him might be sufficient," Constance offered.

"At the very least the man deserves to hear the whole truth," Sir Richard added. "I did not succeed in overhearing everything in that library, but I gather you were not completely candid with the fellow."

Katherine sighed. "No, I let him think I was trying to trap him into marriage for myself. That was wrong of me. I wanted him to see me for myself, but in the end I suspect I simply could not bear him to reject me for myself."

"I shall speak to him," Constance said bravely. "I will tell him the truth. He knows I have no reason to lie."

"I rather think he suspects we all lied to him," Katherine pointed out. "Oh, I made a mull of things!"

Before anyone could comment further, Bixby dashed back into the room, panting. He held out a sealed note to Sir Richard.

"From the War Office," he managed to gasp. "Urgent. That's his nib's own hand. The fellow who brought it wouldn't wait for a reply."

Frowning, Sir Richard stepped away to break the seal.

Katherine exchanged glances with Constance and Emma. She saw in their gazes that they knew something was wrong as well. "Eric," she said, "why don't you go downstairs with Emma and see if you can find some sweets for tea."

"Aw, I never get to hear the good stuff," he complained, but Emma chuckled, took his hand, and led him out.

Katherine stepped to her uncle with Constance beside her. "Bad news?"

"The worst." He turned to sweep them all with his gaze, and Katherine caught her breath at the concern written there. "Hastings promised to let me know if he had reason to suspect Lord Borin of espionage," her uncle explained. "This note was to tell me that

Borin has been called to the War Office for questioning."

Katherine threw up her hands. "They cannot suspect him of this spy business."

Sir Richard met her outraged gaze. "They suspect him," he replied, "of treason."

Twenty-one

Alex leaned back in the leather armchair in the Marquis of Hastings's private office in Whitehall. He did not dare consult the pocket watch in his tastefully embroidered celestial blue waistcoat. Besides, he was certain that time had stood still since he had received the summons.

Lord Hastings gave him no clue to his thoughts. The marquis's deep brown eyes, however, remained on Alex's face. Alex felt the seconds ticking off. He heard Davis Laughton, who stood guard behind the marquis, shift impatiently in his brown coat.

"I regret, my boy," Lord Hastings said, "that I can no longer rely simply on your word as a gentleman that you are not involved with this foreign spy affair. We have a note swearing to your involvement."

Alex reminded himself to remain cool. Losing his temper had nearly cost him Katherine. Losing it now could cost him his life. "And who gave you this note?" he asked Hastings. "Am I not allowed to know the name of my accuser?"

Hastings was equally calm. "Normally, yes. However, the note came anonymously. I hope to shortly learn the name of its originator, but at the moment, it is all we have to go on."

"Yet you accept the word of this unknown person over mine?" Alex tried to keep his tone level, but his irritation must have been evident, for Hastings sighed.

"Dashed irregular, I grant you," the marquis said, "but we are faced with dire times. Napoleon is getting desperate with his recent losses on the Peninsula and the Austrian front. If you believe even half of the rumors circulating, we have spies everywhere."

"I am sorry for the difficulties that must present you," Alex replied. "But surely you know me well enough to vouch for my honor."

"On other occasions I would be only too delighted. But this particular report is quite damaging. It is specific, and concerns information we know for a fact has reached the French."

Even though he knew himself to be innocent, Alex could not help chilling. "Someone seeks to deflect the blame from himself to me," he reasoned.

"Quite possible," Hastings agreed. "Allow me to ask you a few questions. I am certain you will clear your name easily and be back to that important appointment with your tailor in no time."

"My blasted tailor isn't that important," Alex muttered, but he nodded for the marquis to continue.

Hastings leaned forward as if by doing so he could smell the truth of Alex's answers. "Have you been approached by anyone suspicious?"

"No."

"Have you hired any new servants?"

"No."

"Is there any reason you might be blackmailed?"

Alex scowled. "None whatsoever."

"What do you recall of the Willstencraft ball?"

He cocked his head. That was an odd question to throw in. The specifics Lord Hastings had spoken of must have to do with the event. He tried to remember anything different, but aside from his interactions with Katherine and her stepsister, it had been no better or worse than any other society event that Season. "Half the *ton* attended," he offered. "The music was tedious, refreshments abysmal. Lady Janice's gown will likely set a new trend in low necklines, though few gentlemen appeared to mind. I imagine a grand time was had by all."

Hastings's gaze bored into him. "You noticed nothing out of the ordinary?"

"Aside from the fact that you had Trevithan and Laughton watching the flock for wolves? No, not really."

He smiled. "Noticed them, did you? Very observant. Did anyone approach you?"

Alex raised a brow. Someone at the ball had passed secrets, then. He was certain it was no one he knew. "I had any number of friends and acquaintances in attendance," he told Hastings. "At one time or another, they each approached me."

"To be sure. Allow me to be more specific. Trevithan reports that twice you disappeared for protracted periods. He confirms that at least once you were out on the terrace, but he could not identify your partner. Care to enlighten me as to what occurred?"

The two periods were obviously when he had been with Miss Templeman and Katherine. He glanced at Davis Laughton. The young spy was examining a thread that held a shiny gold button to his chamois waistcoat. He acted as if he had no interest in the conversation, although Alex was certain he was listening to every word. Surely he was used to keeping state secrets. Would he value a lady's reputation as highly? Alex wasn't sure he could take the chance.

"I was with a lady," he replied to Hastings. "Surely you will understand that I cannot say more."

Hastings's face was grave. "And I am certain *you* will understand that I cannot let you hide behind that excuse."

"Then perhaps I should find another," Alex quipped. "My memory is foggy, my lord. I do not recall what I did or with whom I did it. The penalty for having entirely too many ladies dangling at once, I fear."

His lordship frowned. "This is no game, Borin. Your ability to tell us what happened during those moments is critical to proving your innocence."

Alex met his gaze in challenge. "And can you promise me that if I tell you all, the *lady's* innocence will remain?"

Hastings shook his head. "I am sorry, but I cannot. We would, of course, have to speak with the lady to corroborate your story."

Knowing Katherine, she would probably be only too delighted to visit the War Office. But her stepsister would also have to visit. If it became known, Alex could imagine the glee Lord Templeman would take in relating the damaging tale to the *ton*. Miss Templeman might never find a suitable husband. He traded his life for hers.

Davis Laughton was watching him, dark eyes thoughtful. Hastings was obviously waiting for him to reply. "Have you nothing to say?" he urged.

Alex squared his shoulders. "Nothing, my lord."

The marquis sighed. "You make things difficult for me, my boy. I will ask you one last time. Knowing that I may have to send you to prison to await trial for treason if you do not answer, where were you and what were you doing during your absence from the Willstencraft ballroom?"

Alex took a deep breath. "I cannot tell you where I was at the Willstencraft ball, my lord. And that is my final word on the subject."

* * *

Of course, Katherine insisted on leaving immediately for the War Office. Sir Richard attempted to dissuade her, but she would have none of it.

"We may not know why they accused him," she argued, "but it may have something to do with his shadow. We know more about the fellow than anyone except Lord Borin. At the very least, we can assure them of his lordship's character."

In the end, Sir Richard could only capitulate. Constance and Bixby also indicated their interest in helping, so the four of them hailed a hack and hurried to the War Office.

Getting to see Lord Hastings, however, proved to be more difficult. Katherine was a little surprised to find that her uncle and Bixby were well-known to many of the senior staff. They were met with salutes and bows wherever they went. It did not take them long to reach the private suite of the Marquis of Hastings. A young captain in an Oxford blue uniform stood guard before the entrance. He too seemed to know Sir Richard, but he refused to let them pass.

"His lordship is in an important meeting," he explained. "I regret that I have been ordered not to disturb him."

"But we have critical information," Sir Richard began in protest. Katherine half listened as she eyed the loyal captain. He stood as tall as her uncle, with short-cropped raven hair and warm brown eyes. The only thing distinguishing him from any other eager captain was a small gold cross half hidden by the black leather baldric on his chest. She had vowed not to manipulate except in a good cause, and surely this was the best. But not knowing the good captain, she was hard-pressed to determine how she might appeal to him.

It was then that she noticed that he too was only half listening to the conversation. His warm smile was all for Constance, who stood at Sir Richard's right elbow. Even more fascinating, however, was the way Constance dimpled at his look of admiration.

Katherine nudged Bixby beside her. Intent on the conversation between Sir Richard and the guard, he started, then turned to her with a frown. She nodded toward the captain and Constance and winked. Bixby followed her gaze, then grinned. She was certain he saw what she did. Katherine nodded again, hoping he would realize that she had a plan and would follow her lead.

The captain continued to offer seemingly sincere apologies. Sir Richard had run out of logic and was blustering, red faced. Katherine stepped easily beside him, laying a hand on his arm. "Oh, dear," she murmured aloud, "it is such a shame we cannot see Lord Hastings. Now we will have to leave London without saying farewell."

Sir Richard frowned. She nodded toward Constance, who was looking up at the guard from under her golden lashes. The captain had cocked his head as if trying to get a better look at her. Her uncle's brow cleared.

"Yes," Sir Richard agreed, "a disappointment, to be sure. Constance, I imagine your heart will be broken. Constance?"

Constance's dimple was showing, and she pursed her lips as she too cocked her head. One gloved hand toyed with the cross around her own neck. The guard winked at her.

"Constance?" Katherine repeated. "Will you not be heartbroken if we do not get to see Lord Hastings immediately?"

Constance blinked and focused on her with obvious

difficulty, causing the guard to start as well. "Heartbroken?" her stepsister asked with a slight frown.

"Yes," Katherine hissed with determination. "I should think it likely that you might even faint."

Constance stared at her; then a slow smile spread. As if realizing someone might notice, she immediately sobered. "Oh, dear," she murmured. "I fear you are right." Her hand fluttered to her brow. "Oh, never to see dear Lord Hastings again. Never to gaze upon his wise brow. Never to hear words of encouragement from his noble mouth. Never to smell the sweet aroma of . . ."

"Yes, dear," Katherine snapped as her stepsister once again warmed to her role, "we know how much you dote upon Lord Hastings. You must try to contain yourself."

"I regret that I cannot allow you entrance," the captain said consolingly. "But 'He that waiteth on his master shall be honored'."

Constance fell immediately out of character, beaming at him. "Proverbs twenty-seven: eighteen," she said. "I used to quote that verse whenever my governess seemed too strict."

Katherine gritted her teeth and nudged her as the captain smiled approvingly. "I think the captain is using it to remind you that we must return later. Is that what you want, Constance?" She could feel Sir Richard and Bixby watching her stepsister as if they held their breaths.

Constance blinked, obviously recalling herself. Her shoulders slumped. "Later?" she breathed, gazing up at the captain as her hand fell limply to her side. "But you do not understand. Later would be entirely too . . . late."

"Precisely," Katherine said. "Now, come away, Constance, before you drive yourself to a complete collapse."

"I . . . I . . ." Constance murmured, eyes rolling back in her head as her voice faded away. "I fear I am beyond help." She crumpled elegantly toward the floor. The captain heroically scooped her up into his arms.

"How very embarrassing," Sir Richard lamented, moving to block the edge of the door from the captain's view. "My niece has such tender sensibilities. I apologize, Captain Randolph."

Bixby took up sentinel on his other side to prevent him from moving away with his burden. "Poor little mite," he murmured, giving Katherine the elbow. "She needs a strong shoulder to lean on."

"Completely understandable," the captain assured them as Sir Richard waved Katherine past behind his back. She did not wait to hear more but slipped inside and closed the door behind her.

She was in a small antechamber. A neat walnut desk and chair stood squarely in her path, but no one sat at it. She could not know whether the captain was its usual occupant or whether its owner was behind the only other door in the room. She tiptoed across the thick blue carpet and leaned her ear against the panel. She could hear nothing from inside. That was not surprising, she supposed. When one led a spy ring, one probably invested in sturdier doors to prevent eavesdropping. She should really look into such doors for their town house.

So, what to do? She was afraid to knock. What if the occupants refused to answer? Worse, what if there was another guard who turned her away? If she wanted to know what was happening, there was only one thing for it. Squaring her shoulders, she pressed down on the handle and opened the door.

And was just in time to hear Alex announce, "I cannot tell you where I was at the Willstencraft ball, my lord, and that is my final word on the subject."

"But not mine," Katherine declared.

The older man behind the walnut desk looked up, and Alex jumped to his feet at the sound of her voice. The only other occupant of the room, a slender gentleman at the back, started forward, but the older man held up his hand to stop him. Then he too rose to confront her.

"Do you have something to add to this conversation, young lady?" he asked politely.

Alex moved to her side, face stern. "She does not. I am certain her interruption was a mistake, wasn't it, madam?"

She met his deep blue gaze and thought she saw concern for her in it. Didn't he know it was far more important for her to save him? She raised her head in determination, then peered around him. "I believe I may have something to say, sir. If I might stay?"

Alex shook his head, then turned to the older man. "My lord, I protest. This was to be a private meeting."

"Then why does he get to be here?" Katherine replied, nodding toward the man at the back of the room.

The older man smiled. "Stand aside, Borin. Let the young lady speak her mind. She appears to be rather good at it."

Ignoring Alex's glare, Katherine scooted around him and spread her gray skirts in a curtsy. "Thank you, my lord. You would be Lord Hastings?"

He bowed. "Your servant, madam. As we are in the middle of a discussion, I shall not introduce my associate. But if I might know your name?"

"It is unimportant," Alex started just as she replied, "Katherine Collins, my lord."

Hastings smiled. "Ah, Sir Richard's niece. You are most welcome, my dear. Won't you sit down?"

Katherine perched on the chair. The unnamed gentleman, whom she assumed must be an arch spy, dragged another chair from the wall and set it beside her, motioning for Alex to sit as well. Alex complied, face hooded. She was sorry to have to go against his wishes, but his life was at stake.

Lord Hastings seated himself behind the desk. "Well, Miss Collins, you have no doubt gone to a great deal of trouble to reach my office and involve yourself in our discussion. Would you care to explain why?"

Katherine nodded. "Certainly, my lord. I understand from my uncle that you believe Lord Borin capable of espionage."

Hastings inclined his head. "That is the charge against him."

"I am amazed you did not dismiss it out of hand," she scolded. "His honor is unassailable."

Hastings managed a polite smile. She thought the man behind him was biting his cheek to prevent laughter. She glared at him.

"We have already taken that into consideration, my dear," Lord Hastings assured her. "I appreciate your passionate defense of the man you love, but I need facts."

Could he tell so easily that she loved Alex? Was her love as emblazoned on her face as it was on her heart? Well, so be it. The time for half-truths and trickery was past. She vowed to tell everything if that would save him. She could feel Alex watching her. She dared not look at him. Would she see censure in those eyes, or hope? Either might make her forget what she had come here to do. She took a deep breath.

"You were discussing the Willstencraft ball when I entered, I believe," she told Lord Hastings. "I was there and watching Lord Borin much of the time. What do you wish to know?"

Twenty-two

"Miss Collins—" Alex started once more.

"Will say what she pleases," Hastings clipped. "If you attempt to stop her again, Borin, I will have you escorted out."

Alex stiffened. "I merely wished to point out," he said tightly, "that Miss Collins should consider her own needs first for once."

Now Katherine stiffened. Her own needs? For once? Did he understand about her War Office then? Had he forgiven her? She had to know. She chanced a look at his eyes and saw love and encouragement written there. Any concerns she had melted away. She smiled at him and saw his mouth curve in a smile in return.

"Miss Collins?" Lord Hastings prompted. "You were going to tell us about the Willstencraft ball?"

She returned her gaze to him with difficulty. "Yes, my lord. As I said, I had Lord Borin in my sights much of the time. What is the question?"

"I will not ask you why you had young Borin under surveillance," he replied knowingly, and she blushed. "What we wish to know is where he disappeared to on two separate occasions, and what he did then."

Katherine blinked. Two occasions. She'd wager she knew exactly what he'd been up to, and why he refused to speak of it himself. "Oh, that is simple. On the first occasion my stepsister invited him out onto the terrace to attempt to compromise him, only he was too noble."

Hastings coughed, and she had a feeling he was trying to hide a laugh. The fellow behind him suddenly found something fascinating in the floor.

"Very commendable," the marquis said. "I had no idea the fellow could resist temptation so admirably. I trust Miss Templeman would be willing to verify your story?"

Katherine nodded. "Very willing. She greatly esteems Lord Borin."

"Yes, very personable fellow, Borin," Hastings quipped. "I had similar reports from any number of young ladies. And what can you tell me about the other occasion?"

"That is easy as well. Part of that time he was with me."

"Busy fellow," Hastings replied, frowning at Alex. "But you said part of the time. Do you know what occurred the other part?"

"Most assuredly." She paused, trying to determine how best to phrase it. Much as she disliked Lord Templeman, she didn't wish to spread gossip, particularly through the War Office. But Lord Hastings was watching her, and she had a feeling he'd see through any screen she attempted to put up. She hurried on. "Lord Templeman, my stepsister's cousin, was attempting to bribe Lord Borin to stay away from Constance."

Hastings blinked as if the answer surprised him. "And how do you know this?"

Now she felt Alex's eyes on her. He was probably thinking she'd eavesdropped. For once, she could say that was not the case. "I saw them return to the ballroom together," she told Lord Hastings, "and I saw the results of the bribe."

Alex shook his head, but by the smile on his face she thought the gesture stemmed from reluctant admiration rather than censure.

"So," Hastings mused, pursing his lips, "Borin accepted a bribe from Templeman?"

Now why did she think he invested Lord Templeman's name with particular interest? Was Constance's cousin more involved in this matter than she had thought? "Actually, Lord Borin did me a favor," Katherine explained. "He was never courting my stepsister. Lord Templeman was mistaken in that regard. Lord Borin knew that Lord Templeman had kept something of mine, and in exchange for supposedly ceasing his suit with Constance, he forced Lord Templeman to return it."

"And this item would be?" Hastings prompted.

"My harp," she said. Beside her, Alex smiled fondly.

"I think I begin to see," Hastings replied. "An interesting story, Miss Collins. You would be willing to swear its truth on your honor?"

"Yes, of course," she agreed. "Lord Borin is no spy, my lord. I would stake my life on it."

Alex reached out to squeeze her hand, and she took joy from the gesture. Surely their problems were over.

Hastings leaned back in his chair. "What else can you tell me about Lord Templeman?"

So, he is interested, Katherine thought. "Only that I like him very little," she replied, but couldn't help adding a question of her own. "Why do you ask?"

"Let us merely say," Lord Hastings replied with a short smile, "that I have taken an interest in him."

Katherine's frown deepened. "Was he the one who accused Lord Borin?"

His dark eyes kindled. "Why would you suspect that?"

Why wouldn't she? A better question would be why

hadn't she seen it sooner? "Only because he was so sure that Lord Borin was the spy," she told Lord Hastings. "He warned me days ago that Lord Borin would be caught for espionage."

Alex frowned. Hastings raised a brow. "Did he, indeed?"

Katherine stared at him, assurance growing with every moment. "He must have intended to implicate Lord Borin all along, the toad! He probably arranged to have Lord Borin followed as well." Another realization hit, and she hopped to her feet. "That's why the shadow went to Miss Montgomery's flat! He was bribing her to tell that ridiculous tale."

"And what tale would that be?" Lord Hastings asked, leaning forward as Alex gazed at Katherine in amazement.

Katherine shook her head. "Nothing about your spy, I promise you. She came to our home to convince Constance that Lord Borin beat her."

"What?" Alex all but yelped, hopping to his feet as well. "Katherine, I swear to you that I—"

"Am innocent," Katherine completed, laying a hand on his chest and gazing up at him. "I know that. You would never bully anyone. You are far too much a gentleman."

The anger drained from his face to be replaced by such a warm smile that her heart turned over.

Lord Hastings cleared his throat. "Have you anything else you'd like to share about your stepsister's cousin, Miss Collins?"

Katherine forced her gaze away from Alex to eye the marquis. "Only that I would very much like to get my hands on him."

"I share your desire, my dear," Lord Hastings assured her. "I believe you can safely leave the matter with me. Lord Borin, Miss Collins, thank you for coming. You are free to go."

Alex stared at Hastings. She'd done it. They were free. He felt his grin spreading as he returned his gaze to Katherine. She smiled up at him. His gaze was drawn to her sweet lips.

Hastings interrupted any further thought. "A moment, Borin, before you go."

Alex turned to him with difficulty. Beside him, Katherine stiffened warily. "My lord?" Alex asked.

Hastings quirked a smile. "You offered your assistance to my Service some time ago. If the offer still stands, I should like to take you up on it."

Alex blinked. "My lord? I thought you felt me unqualified."

"Certain actions have come to my ears," Hastings replied. "I amend my earlier opinion. We'd be pleased to have you."

He'd been accepted! His heart leaped at the thought. Alex opened his mouth to accept and felt Katherine's hand tighten in his own. Glancing down at her, he saw her smiling tremulously. Why did he need to accept Hastings to give his life meaning? All his hopes and dreams, everything he might become, was standing beside him. He shook his head.

"I am sorry, Hastings, but I must decline. I hope to be married shortly and would like to devote myself to my bride."

Katherine's cheeks reddened, but he saw the answer glowing from her eyes.

"I see," Hastings replied with a chuckle. "I would be willing to offer you a place as well, Miss Collins. You have a great deal of your uncle in you. However, I suspect I shall get the same answer."

Alex held his breath. Here was a use for her considerable talents. He'd always thought she'd make a better agent than he would. Hastings no doubt hoped they would serve together, but Alex didn't think he could function as an agent knowing that Katherine might be in danger. But could he stand to be left behind if she accepted?

She smiled at him, not even bothering to turn toward Lord Hastings. "I fear you are right about my answer, my lord," she replied readily. "I too hope to be wed shortly and would like to devote myself to my husband."

Alex blew out a breath. Despite the audience, he could do no more than pull her into his arms.

Katherine cared nothing for the audience either. All she knew was that Alex loved her, wanted her, was willing to give up a life of intrigue to marry her. She had no more doubts, no more fears. She felt his love for her and her own love growing with it. She could not have asked for more.

Beside them, she heard Lord Hastings chuckle. "If you meant to keep your love a secret, Borin, you're doing a dashed poor job of it."

Alex raised his head, but kept her close as if afraid to lose her. She made no move to leave his arms, finding them all too comfortable.

"It is no secret, my lord," he told the marquis. "You see the happiest man on earth."

"And the happiest woman," Katherine assured him.

"Well, if they won't accept a position," Sir Richard declared from the doorway, "I will."

"Did you all overcome my guard," Lord Hastings demanded, "or was he carried away by gypsies?"

"Neither," Sir Richard replied, moving into the room with a nod toward Laughton, who was shaking his head. "Though I suspect him shortly to carry off my ward in marriage, by the way they are crooning over each other."

"Blasted epidemic," Hastings complained, though there was a twinkle in his dark eyes. "Just like this spying. Send them on their way, Richard, and we can talk."

"Your servant, sir," he replied, putting a hand on Alex's shoulder and pushing him toward the door. "Send Bixby to me, and see that my wards get safely home, won't you, Borin?"

"With pleasure, sir," Alex assured him.

Out in the antechamber, he slowed his steps, savoring a few moments alone with Katherine. She did not complain, lingering with him before the door.

"Have you truly forgiven me?" she murmured, enfolding one of his hands with her own.

He used his free hand to trace her cheek with one finger. "There is nothing to forgive. You did what you felt you must to save your family. I admire your courage and your foresight in carrying out the plan. Do you forgive me for thinking you were anything but marvelous?"

A tear trickled down her cheek, and he caught it with his finger. "Tears?"

"Happy tears," she replied with a sniff. "And there is also no need to forgive you. You had every right to be angry with me. I used my talents to disadvantage. I promise not to manipulate you again, Alex. But I fear I shall always be a managing female. It seems to be in my blood."

He smiled. "I have a great number of activities that need managing, my dear. Your considerable skills will not go to waste. In fact, I have a task for you right now."

She cocked her head. "Oh?"

He grinned and placed a quick kiss on her ear before

whispering, "Yes. Can you manage to find a way to occupy your stepsister once we return to your town house so we may have some time together?"

She smiled back. "For you, Lord Borin, I can manage anything."

Dear Reader,

I hope you enjoyed the story of Alex and Katherine. I must admit to being a managing female myself. It wasn't until a fellow Christian pointed out that my administrative skills were a gift, that I was able to convince myself, and my husband, that "plan" isn't a four-letter word.

I hope you also enjoyed seeing old friends from my other stories. Kevin Whattling, Giles Sloan, and Sir Nigel Dillingham are featured in *The Bluestocking on His Knee,* where the boxing-mad Mr. Whattling meets his match in heiress Eugennia Welch. Allison Munroe, with whom Constance drives instead of meeting with Alex, almost married the Marquis DeGuis in *Catch of the Season.* However, that handsome marquis, who partners Constance for two dances at the Willstencraft ball, tried courting the emerald-eyed Lady Janice, but found that his kiss was more appropriate for Margaret Munroe in *The Marquis' Kiss.* Ultra-confident spies Davis Laughton and Allister Fenwick, Baron Trevithan, battled for England, and the love of Allister's life, Joanna Lindby, in "The June Bride Conspiracy" in the anthology *His Blushing Bride.*

I love to hear from readers. Please visit my Web site at www.reginascott.com or e-mail me at regina@reginascott.com. If you send me a letter via Zebra, please enclose a self-addressed, stamped envelope if you would like a reply.

Happy reading!
Regina Scott

Celebrate Romance With One of Today's Hottest Authors

Amanda Scott

__**Border Bride**
0-8217-7000-4 $5.99US/$7.99CAN

__**Border Fire**
0-8217-6586-8 $5.99US/$7.99CAN

__**Border Storm**
0-8217-6762-3 $5.99US/$7.99CAN

__**Dangerous Lady**
0-8217-6113-7 $5.99US/$7.50CAN

__**Dangerous Illusions**
0-7860-1078-9 $5.99US/$7.99CAN

__**Highland Fling**
0-8217-5816-0 $5.99US/$7.50CAN

__**Highland Spirits**
0-8217-6343-1 $5.99US/$7.99CAN

__**Highland Treasure**
0-8217-5860-8 $5.99US/$7.50CAN

Call toll free **1-888-345-BOOK** to order by phone or use this coupon to order by mail.

Name_____

Address_____

City_____ State_____ Zip_____

Please send me the books I have checked above.

I am enclosing	$_____
Plus postage and handling*	$_____
Sales tax (in New York and Tennessee)	$_____
Total amount enclosed	$_____

*Add $2.50 for the first book and $.50 for each additional book.

Send check or money order (no cash or CODs) to: **Kensington Publishing Corp., 850 Third Avenue, New York, NY 10022**

Prices and numbers subject to change without notice. All orders subject to availability.

Check out our website at **www.kensingtonbooks.com.**

The Queen of Romance

Cassie Edwards

__Desire's Blossom 0-8217-6405-5	$5.99US/$7.99CAN
__Exclusive Ecstasy 0-8217-6597-3	$5.99US/$7.99CAN
__Passion's Web 0-8217-5726-1	$5.99US/$7.50CAN
__Portrait of Desire 0-8217-5862-4	$5.99US/$7.50CAN
__Savage Obsession 0-8217-5554-4	$5.99US/$7.50CAN
__Silken Rapture 0-8217-5999-X	$5.99US/$7.50CAN
__Rapture's Rendezvous 0-8217-6115-3	$5.99US/$7.50CAN

Call toll free **1-888-345-BOOK** to order by phone or use this coupon to order by mail.

Name_____

Address_____

City_____ State _____ Zip _____

Please send me the books that I have checked above.

I am enclosing	$_____
Plus postage and handling*	$_____
Sales tax (in New York and Tennessee)	$_____
Total amount enclosed	$_____

*Add $2.50 for the first book and $.50 for each additional book. Send check or money order (no cash or CODs) to:

Kensington Publishing Corp., 850 Third Avenue, New York, NY 10022

Prices and numbers subject to change without notice.

All orders subject to availability.

Check out our website at **www.kensingtonbooks.com**.

Celebrate Romance With
Meryl Sawyer

__Thunder Island $6.99US/$8.99CAN
0-8217-6378-4

__Half Moon Bay $6.50US/$8.00CAN
0-8217-6144-7

__The Hideaway $5.99US/$7.50CAN
0-8217-5780-6

__Tempting Fate $6.50US/$8.00CAN
0-8217-5858-6

__Trust No One $6.99US/$8.99CAN
0-8217-6676-7

Call toll free **1-888-345-BOOK** to order by phone, use this coupon to order by mail, or order online at **www.kensingtonbooks.com**.
Name_____
Address_____
City_____ State _____ Zip _____
Please send me the books I have checked above.
I am enclosing $_____
Plus postage and handling* $_____
Sales tax (in New York and Tennessee only) $_____
Total amount enclosed $_____
*Add $2.50 for the first book and $.50 for each additional book.
Send check or money order (no cash or CODs) to:
Kensington Publishing Corp., Dept. C.O., 850 Third Avenue, New York, NY 10022
Prices and numbers subject to change without notice.
All orders subject to availability.
Visit our website at **www.kensingtonbooks.com**.

More Zebra Regency Romances

__A Taste for Love by Donna Bell $4.99US/$6.50CAN
    0-8217-6104-8

__An Unlikely Father by Lynn Collum $4.99US/$6.99CAN
    0-8217-6418-7

__An Unexpected Husband by Jo Ann Ferguson $4.99US/$6.99CAN
    0-8217-6481-0

__Wedding Ghost by Cindy Holbrook $4.99US/$6.50CAN
    0-8217-6217-6

__Lady Diana's Darlings by Kate Huntington $4.99US/$6.99CAN
    0-8217-6655-4

__A London Flirtation by Valerie King $4.99US/$6.99CAN
    0-8217-6535-3

__Lord Langdon's Tutor by Laura Paquet $4.99US/$6.99CAN
    0-8217-6675-9

__Lord Mumford's Minx by Debbie Raleigh $4.99US/$6.99CAN
    0-8217-6673-2

__Lady Serena's Surrender by Jeanne Savery $4.99US/$6.99CAN
    0-8217-6607-4

__A Dangerous Dalliance by Regina Scott $4.99US/$6.99CAN
    0-8217-6609-0

__Lady May's Folly by Donna Simpson $4.99US/$6.99CAN
    0-8217-6805-0

Call toll free **1-888-345-BOOK** to order by phone or use this coupon to order by mail.

Name_____

Address_____

City_____ State_____ Zip_____

Please send me the books I have checked above.

I am enclosing $_____

Plus postage and handling* $_____

Sales tax (in New York and Tennessee only) $_____

Total amount enclosed $_____

*Add $2.50 for the first book and $.50 for each additional book.

Send check or money order (no cash or CODs) to:

Kensington Publishing Corp., 850 Third Avenue, New York, NY 10022

Prices and numbers subject to change without notice.

All orders subject to availability.

Check out our website at **www.kensingtonbooks.com**.